I0579435

Jinxers

Sabrina Chase

CONTENTS

Also by Sabrina Chase

Firehearted
The Scent of Metal
The Bureau of Substandards Annual Report

THE SEQUOYAH TRILOGY:
The Long Way Home
Raven's Children
Queen of Chaos

GUARDIAN'S COMPACT:
The Last Mage Guardian
Dragonhunters

ACKNOWLEDGMENTS

Many thanks to the beta readers who helped with Jinxers!
Some young, some young at heart. As always, my
profound gratitude to the fine folks of STEW, supreme
editor and comma-herder Deb Taber, and proofreader of
great skill Roger Ivie. My books are all the better for your
help.

CHAPTER 1
A WORLD OF TROUBLE

Jin skulked out of sight behind a group of grimy dockworkers, waiting for the noisy crowd in front of the burned building to leave. With a stab of fear, he recognized one of the voices in the crowd and ducked into the shadows, not daring even to look. Ogney had been looking for him for months, suspicious that Jin had been the one to take Mr. Andel's money. He'd beat Jin bloody just to find out. Maybe the alley would be safer instead. Jin had to get inside the building soon, and Ogney was in no hurry to go anywhere.

The alley was empty, and even better, had a gutter pipe still mostly attached to the brick wall. Jin glanced around and climbed as quickly and quietly as he could to a thick piece of stone trim, and from there to an empty window. The wood frame was charred. Inside, nothing remained of the old warehouse but rubble and ash. A beam had fallen near the window, one end resting on a pile of fallen brick from the upper stories and the other down near the middle of the building. He could just reach it with his toes if he dangled from the windowsill.

Jin shivered and forced himself forward, stepping carefully on the charred beam. The smell of smoke was strong enough to make him cough, and he muffled his face in the crook of his arm. He had to hurry—the light was fading fast in the sky, and he could barely feel his feet anymore. The rags he'd tied around them were not enough to keep them warm. If he still had his hidey-hole in the stables it wouldn't matter so much, but thanks to the fire, he didn't. He hadn't even been able to grab the ratty wool blanket he'd kept there or the few pennies he'd saved. He had nothing but the clothes he wore on his back.

Jin took another step and his foot slipped on a hidden layer of ice under the ash. The beam shifted with a thud, and Jin froze in fear. If anyone heard, they might come nosing around. He wasn't stealing; not really. Taking things nobody wanted anymore wasn't stealing. Even Mr. Andel said so. Before the fire the warehouse had been empty and abandoned for years. The billies might nab him for a rab anyway, though. Some of them thought he stole, when he really was just good at finding things. He didn't want to give them any reason to think it harder. Besides, if nobody knew he was there, they couldn't make him leave before he found what he was looking for.

Fear made him move again. The soot-covered skeletal brick walls were still sharp against the evening sky, but soon they would all blend together in darkness. The roof was completely gone and most of the few windows broken by the fire brigade. He had to find something, anything, valuable enough to sell. Old Coffers under the bridge wouldn't let Jin stay by the fire for the night unless he paid. If he didn't get warm, he would die. He tucked his fingers, numb with cold, under his arms and ignored the hollow ache in his stomach. He'd been hungry before. You just couldn't let it get to you, that's all.

No, he wasn't stealing. The fire had destroyed everything he had, so it was only fair the old warehouse give up a few dibs in return. And best of all, the gobbers and door-fumblers like Ogney and Thumbless Bode wouldn't give it a second look. Nothing for them in a burned-out building.

Jin, however, had read the faded, peeling letters on the brick front while he watched the fire with the rest of the street folk. *Vanter Exotics Co.* Even if Ogney and Bode could read, it wouldn't have meant much to them. But Jin had heard about Vanter from Mr. Andel many times, so he knew how they got their exotic goods. They had been jinxers, some of the very first.

Jinxers could make things out of magic, things that had never existed before in all of Galetan. Everybody knew they could make fiery gems and gold silk that glowed with light, all with magic. The way Mr. Andel talked about them, besides knowing how to make rare treasures, they liked hiding things. Just like Mr. Andel had. Maybe Vanter had cleared out when they moved shop years ago, but people forgot stuff all the time. Maybe Jin wouldn't find gold silk or gems, but something valuable enough he could sleep where it was warm. Something that didn't burn.

But where to look? If anything had survived the fire, it would likely be near the walls. Jin moved rough iron brackets, twisted with heat, stirring up ash that covered his face, tasting dry and sour. A section of brick wall had fallen nearby, and he used a length of iron rod as a lever to shift it. The piles of ash and cinders yielded nothing of value, only a few bent and pitted nails. They snapped when Jin tried to straighten them, and he gave up. Even the tinkers wouldn't give him anything for that.

He kept going. The glint of metal caught his eye, making his heart pound. Yellow metal. Just under a big piece of stone with fancy carving round the edge. It must have come from the roof, then. Jin dug a bit more, getting excited. It looked like the nozzle of a fire hose that had gotten trapped when the stone trim fell. It was brass and nearly as long as his forearm. Watchmakers paid good coin for brass, and if he went down by the river, he could find one that wouldn't ask how a ragged boy like him came by a bit of firefighter's gear.

He couldn't work it free. The stone piece had landed on a section of concrete, trapping the nozzle, and he couldn't dig underneath. The stone itself was much too heavy for him to even budge, although he tried every way he could. Jin hunkered down, staring at the battered piece of brass that was so tantalizingly close.

Maybe he could break a piece free. Or smash a bit of the concrete floor and get it out that way. It would make noise, but that wasn't the real problem. He wasn't sure he had the strength to do it. It was harder to think, to even care. His fingers weren't working like they should. The brass was valuable enough to feed him and keep him warm for days, but it was useless where it was. He had to find something else.

Get up. Keep moving. It took everything he had to stand again, and to move. If only he could stop, just for a minute. If only the fire had started in the evening instead of the morning. He'd have had a chance to rescue his things, and he could have kept warm tonight. But there wouldn't have been a need for a lantern at the stables during the day, and he'd heard a fallen lantern had started it, landing in the straw.

No luck. No luck at all.

Now it felt like pins stabbing him everywhere when he moved. Jin shuffled his feet in the loose debris, hoping to uncover something that way. He felt so dizzy he was afraid he would fall if he bent over to lift anything, and his heart was beating so hard it felt like it was shaking him.

Maybe he was dying.

Fear shivered through him. He couldn't die now. He had to...he had to get better first. You could make up for bad things you'd done if you tried real hard and meant it. Mr. Andel had told him that. But if Jin died now, before making it better, well, he'd go to hell, wouldn't he? He wouldn't see Mr. Andel there, he was sure. And Mr. Andel would feel sad and wouldn't enjoy heaven as much. Jin didn't want to disappoint him like that.

He took another careful step, but his foot snagged on something hidden in the ash and cinders and he fell hard. Jin felt a little warmer and wondered if some of the fire still burned. Maybe he could dig in, stay here overnight?

No. It isn't really warm. You just can't feel the wind, that's all.

Jin struggled to get back on his feet, grabbing anything in reach to pull himself up. The black shape he gripped wasn't a block of stone as he had thought, though. It rocked, creaking. Wood. Big as a door, but thick, and lying on its side. He managed to get his feet back under him and stood, finally making sense of what it was. A cabinet? It was charred all over and had metal locks on the doors, top and bottom.

If he could get the locks out, that might be enough. Worth more with the keys, of course, but the river dealers knew how to make replacements. Jin shoved the cabinet over hard, onto a patch of concrete. It landed with a smash, shattering and stirring up a cloud of ash. Someone would definitely hear that. He needed to move fast.

Jin ripped the doors open, the wood crumbling in his hands. Inside he could see big flakes of grey ash and fragments of paper, too small to read anything. He pulled one of the iron locks free from the door and stuffed it in a pocket. He rummaged through the debris inside, pricking his fingers on what turned out to be a handful of brass brads, like leather bank boxes had. Maybe the papers inside had been valuable—but then, someone like Jin would never be able to sell those without trouble.

He tugged at the second set of doors. This lock took more effort to free, and the wood was more sturdy here. The inside was full of charred material, and he pulled it free to get a better look in the fading light.

Jin heard a faint ping as something fell and hit the ground. A coin?

He scrabbled in the rough ash, feeling the smooth surface before he saw it. Not a coin—something round. He pulled it out, almost dropping it when he saw the bright, fiery gleam inside. But it wasn't a coal —the little crystal sphere looked like it held a flame, surrounded by a suspended swirl of tiny flecks of gold. Jin stared at it agape, marveling at its perfection. He wasn't sure what it was, but it *had* to be valuable.

He should have been running by now. Someone would have heard the noise. He had two metal locks, enough to get him a warm place to sleep and a little food. The little sphere was extra. Jin knew he should go, but he could not tear his eyes away. It was strange, the more he stared, the more the sphere seemed to glow and burn and...get larger. There was a humming noise he could feel in his bones, soothing and numbing his fear.

A warm gust of wind hit his chilled face and made his hands tingle. Jin frowned, puzzled. The warm air smelled strange, dry and hot and like the bakery shop when they made ginger drops.

And then he looked away from the sphere in his fingers. There *was* something larger in front of him, glowing. It was round, like the crystal sphere, and taller than he was. It looked like a magic lantern scene, bright and mysterious, but not any of the usual subjects Jin had seen, such as the Caerdon Crown castle or famous battles. What was the brownish block in the distance? Why was the ground bare and empty? Then he realized this wasn't a lantern show. Even the best of them didn't have warm air like that, or scents. *It's magic. Jinxer magic.*

The crystal sphere made heat; that was clear. Now he could make it warm wherever he wanted! Jin went closer to the picture, sagging in relief. He'd just get warm first, then find somewhere safe to sleep. Where the light wouldn't get seen, maybe under the docks. In the morning he would sell the locks and keep looking here. Maybe he'd find more jinxer gear.

Hot air kept streaming from the picture. Jin smiled and shuffled closer. And tripped. And fell.

Fell on hot sand.

The crystal sphere fell from his hand and rolled away. Jin snatched it back up and looked over his shoulder. A dark hole slowly shrank in midair and vanished with a crackling hiss. Directly overhead, a bright sun hung in a pure blue sky, without a cloud to be seen. A vast expanse of sand surrounded him. No burned warehouse, no ash, no snow.

Jin sat up, more frightened than ever. It wasn't a picture. And he wasn't in Thama anymore.

CHAPTER 2
MORE LOST THAN USUAL

At least he wasn't cold. Jin tried to be glad, but the truth was he was in just as much trouble as before—it was just a different kind of trouble. Sure, he was in no danger of freezing here, but he just might melt.

He'd found some wooden boards half-buried in the sand, a few bricks, and part of a staircase. The wood was bleached from the sun, rough and warped with age. If there had been a building here, it was a long time ago. He also found some empty tins, one with a picture of a milkmaid and a few words in Caerda. Everything else was sand.

He wiped sweat from his face with his ragged sleeve, then stopped and took off his coat. That felt so much better he sat down and untied the rags knotted around his feet, but after a few steps on burning-hot sand, he put some of them back on again.

While he was doing that motion caught his attention from the corner of his eye. Jin jerked his head around, ready to run, but it was just a little creature, not even as big as a dock rat, just a few feet away. It was long and thin, with two stiff, crinkled ridges side by side on its back. Its skin glistened black, like a piece of broken coal, with a pattern of thin red lines all over. It had red eyes, too, which were staring at Jin as intently as he was staring at the creature.

Jin sneezed, and the creature sprang up in the air, wings unfolding with a snap. He snatched at it, but it was too fast, pinwheeling away into the sky. Jin ran after it but gave up after a few steps. He was still weak, and the heat was making it even worse. The sun was so bright he could barely see.

Maybe he could find the creature again and tame it. It looked like it was smart enough to learn tricks, too. There was an old crippled man near the fish market that had a trained squirrel that did tricks, and people threw pennies just to see it fetch them and put them in the man's pockets.

Jin sighed and looked back the way he had come. That was in Thama, though, and he didn't know how to get back. He licked his lips, tasting salt sweat. They were starting to crack in the dry heat. What should he do now?

He was hungry, and he wanted to get out of the sun. The brownish block he had seen—maybe it was a building. With people. For lack of a better option, he started walking that direction. He could see darker shapes on the horizon, farther off. He'd heard of mountains, but living in the city of Thama all his life, had never seen any. Except in a picture, once. Those mountains had white snow on the top, and these didn't.

Maybe he had died after all, and he was in hell. That would explain the heat, but surely hell wouldn't be so...boring? And he still had the two iron locks, and—he checked with a panicked feeling—the little crystal sphere with the flame. Those had been real, and they still were. But if he wasn't dead, where was he? And where could he find water?

Thama had a big river running through it, and fog

and rain most of the year. It had never occurred to Jin, living in Thama his entire short life, that water was something you could run out of. The light was starting to make his head hurt, and it was still impossibly hot, so he took off his shirt and twisted it over and around his head like a hood. It helped a little, and kept the sun off his eyes.

Jin stumbled up a slope and stopped at the top, trying to understand what he was seeing. The brownish block was still off in the distance, but below him was a series of square pillars, the same color as the sand, strung out in a ragged line. They had windows at the top, with what looked like shutters. He didn't see anything that looked like a real house, or even roads or carts or people, but people must be around somewhere, and maybe some of them had water.

He staggered down to the flat area with the towers, feeling dizzy. At least he wasn't dripping sweat anymore, which stung when it got in his eyes. If he couldn't find water, perhaps he could find some shade. Circling the first tower, Jin was puzzled to find it had no door. The only openings he could see were the shuttered windows at the very top, which rattled a bit in the wind that came down the slope. He tried shouting, but his throat was too dry to produce much more than a weak yell.

He tried another tower, and another. Still no doors. The towers were made of a flaky, porous brick with hardly any mortar. Some had bands of cut patterns near the base or wood posts that protruded just below the windows. Nothing he could pound on that would make any noise.

Now his dizziness was making it hard for him to

walk. The shadows at the bases of the towers were lengthening, long enough for him to lie down in them, so he did. What could he do now? If there were people here, they couldn't hear him, and he couldn't yell louder without water. Maybe they were looking out the windows, though. If he waved his coat, they might notice.

Jin leaned against the wall and pushed himself to his feet again, struggling to lift his coat. It was so heavy...

He blinked. The locks. He'd forgotten completely about them. He didn't have to pound on the walls; he could hit the locks together!

He smashed the locks, one in each hand, until they made a loud clang. Then he started to get dizzy again, and Jin collapsed in the shade, managing to lift one lock up and drop it on the other, lying on the ground. Again, and again, and again.

It was hard to open his eyes. They felt dry and full of sand. How strange—the towers were dark now and had gotten closer. He had thought they were taller, though. And...not moving. These towers moved.

They moved until they surrounded him, too weak to move, and their walls rustled and flowed about them in dark clouds, clouds that became larger until they swallowed Jin whole.

* * *

The vision in his mind was blurry but slowly cleared. He was in Mr. Andel's room in the boardinghouse, with sunlight streaming through the open window. Mr. Andel was sitting in his armchair with the old red blanket over his frail legs even though the day was warm. Jin felt a jolt of unexpected happiness at seeing the old man, and then wondered why he was so surprised. Mr. Andel was always in his room. Maybe he'd thought he would be in bed and not feeling well—but there he was, his eyes crinkling at the corners as they did when he was smiling inside.

"Let's have the box, lad."

Jin knew exactly what he meant. He darted over to the other window in the wall, the one that had been bricked up to save money on the window tax. One brick could be pulled out, if you knew how to push down on the wood sill that still remained, and behind that was a space backed by the layer of brick that formed the exterior of the boardinghouse. His small fingers found the carved wood box and brought it over to Mr. Andel.

"There. Quarter-day, and we make good any small depredations." His thin, shaking fingers opened an oilcloth bag from inside the box and counted the gold coins it held, adding a few more from his pocket. "A proper funeral, with a marker and a coffin," he said softly, as he always did. A scattering of silver and copper coins rattled about the box on their own, and Mr. Andel selected a few of them. "A mug of porter, Jin, and I think one of the meat pies the Ship and Anchor does so well. I'm feeling hungry today."

Jin took the coins and ran down the stairs to the inn across the street, relaying the order to the untidy maid inside. He had to balance the hot pie, wrapped in a napkin, on top of the mug in order to carry it back, his mouth watering at the rich, meaty smell. This happened every quarter-day. Mr. Andel would drink the porter and nibble on the pie, exclaiming how good it was, and then say he was too full and invite Jin to finish, "before it gets cold."

Jin always did. He loved quarter-day and Mr.

Andel's quiet, whispery voice telling him stories while he ate. And then, if the light was still good, Mr. Andel would select a volume from the small bookcase by his bedside and invite Jin to read to him.

Mr. Andel was the only person Jin knew who had a special chair just for reading in, and actual books he owned. Jin had always been curious about the books, and Mr. Andel had patiently showed him what they were—and taught him how to read them. Jin struggled with the longer, complicated words that had no real meaning to him, and Mr. Andel praised his efforts. Sometimes it almost made sense. He liked the poems best, because they were like the songs sung in the taproom of the inn, which told stories of adventures and battles and far-off lands.

And then...and then the vision changed, even though Jin fought to keep it from changing. He didn't want to remember this part. The light was pale and grey through the window, and frost covered the panes. Mr. Andel was lying in his bed, hands folded and eyes closed in his sunken face. Closed forever. He still had that small smile at the corners of his mouth, even in death, and Jin knew why. Mr. Andel still had his funeral fund and would be buried properly, not dumped in an unmarked pauper's grave as he had feared.

He heard voices on the stairs and the tramp of heavy feet, and with a stab of fear, Jin remembered why he was here. Ogney had heard rumors of Mr. Andel's box, and the rumors had grown in the telling to a vast sum of gold. The landlord had left the boardinghouse to fetch the coroner, and Ogney had seen an opportunity to take what he could find.

Jin scrambled for the hidden box. He snatched the

oilcloth bag out and jammed the box back in the hole, leaving the brick slightly protruding, and slid under the bare metal bedframe just as the door opened.

Thick boots trod carefully in the room, and Jin held his breath. There weren't many places to hide anything in Mr. Andel's room, but Ogney ransacked them all, tossing the books to the floor and pulling everything from the wardrobe.

Eventually he saw the loose brick. As soon as Jin heard him pull it free with a scrape, he crawled out the other side of the bed and darted for the door.

Ogney cursed under his breath, but as Jin had hoped, didn't follow immediately. Ogney thought he had the money, and only when he discovered the few coins left did he give chase—and Jin was faster.

He ran out of the building and into the crowd before Ogney saw him, and didn't stop running until he reached his destination, a severe, stately building with a brass plate on the door. *Kovles and Son, Undertakers.*

Jin went to the back door. He'd been thinking of what he should say as he ran, knowing that customers would go in the front, but not a ragged street boy.

"I been sent by a gentleman," he said to the somewhat surprised servant that opened the door when he knocked. Now, how was it that Mr. Andel had said it? "To...to make arrangements for a burial. It's all wrote out on a paper inside." He handed the servant the oilskin bag. "Is it enough?"

His running had made him hot, even though ice and snow covered the ground. The servant looked at him with a frown. "Yes, it is enough."

Jin turned to go. Maybe Ogney would not learn he was the one who had paid the undertaker. He'd suspect Jin had taken the money, though. Everyone knew Mr. Andel trusted Jin.

"Aren't you forgetting something?"

Jin stopped. *No. That's not what happened. Why is this different?* The stones under his feet were burning hot.

"Taking what does not belong to you is theft. And thieves," the voice hissed, "*are punished.*"

Fire engulfed him in searing pain. His skin was blistering, charring. Jin screamed and tried to run, but something had trapped his legs, and they could barely move.

"I had to do it!" he cried. "It's what he wanted!"

And then there was a feeling of coolness, the fresh scent of crushed herbs, and a calm, soft voice that soothed his fear, even though he couldn't understand what it was saying. The fire died back, and Jin let go —falling into unconsciousness.

CHAPTER 3
DARK WATER

Jin woke in darkness. He could hear a trickling, gurgling noise to one side—the sound of running water—and the air smelled like herbs. He had dreamed of water, cool and refreshing. Perhaps this was another dream? He could feel a breeze on his face, which was hot and sore. When he touched his cheek, a dried crust crumbled away and the herb smell was even stronger. Did he have a fever? Had he gotten sick? His head was throbbing, and it was hard to think.

Then he remembered. The burned warehouse, the hot sand, the towers with no doors. Where was he? Why did his chest and back feel like they were on fire?

He managed to move, painfully turning on his side. A flickering light came from a niche above him, with a darker shadow to one side. On his other side came the sound of the running water, and the breeze was strongest there. He was lying on a thin mat, covered by a length of damp fabric—and all of his clothes were gone.

Jin sat up despite the searing pain that made him yelp. The crystal sphere—it was gone!

More details emerged from the gloom as his eyes adapted. The wall near him was made of stone blocks, and the surface under him was rock, too, but all one piece. Had the billies caught him and put him in jail?

But where were the chains, then?

The glimmering reflection off to one side must be the water he was hearing. He sank back on one elbow and cautiously stuck his hand out. Ice-cold water moved past his fingers, and he scooped some up to drink. He'd never heard of a jail with a stream in it.

The sound of footsteps alerted him. Jin wanted to run, but he wasn't sure he could stand—and if he was dead, or in prison, it wouldn't do any good. Something wooden shifted and creaked, and from the darker patch of shadow a human figure emerged, swathed in dark fabric from head to foot. Small sparks of gold on the fabric caught the light from a lamp. All Jin could see of the person were eyes, which widened slightly when they caught sight of him.

"H—hello," Jin managed to say, although his throat felt dry despite the water. "Is this a prison?"

The figure darted away, and he heard the shifting sound of wood again. Several minutes passed, and then he heard footsteps again. This time two people appeared, the one he had seen before and another, shorter one wearing red and yellow with a carelessly tossed black scarf about her face, thin as smoke. A girl? She spoke, and the other person answered, her voice revealing her to be an older woman.

Jin shrank back and attempted to pull the thin sheet completely over himself. He *really* wished he knew where his clothes were.

The girl came closer, staring intently at his face. He stared too. Jin had never seen anyone with skin so brown or such angry dark eyes.

"What are you doing here?" the girl said. Jin felt his jaw drop. The words sounded strange, but he understood them.

"I don't know...I was in the burned-out warehouse on Pinnaker Street." Both of them stared at him with blank, puzzled expressions. "North of the river docks? In the city of Thama?" The puzzled expressions remained. "Um, anyway, I was in this place and...then I wasn't, and it was all hot and bright and nothing but sand...and now I'm in a...tunnel?"

The dark eyes narrowed. "When did you leave the fort? Why are they not seeking you?"

"What fort?"

They stared at each other in mutual confusion. The woman said something that sounded like a question in a soft voice. The girl answered, and this time Jin didn't understand what she said. A foreigner! He'd heard the sailors who visited the Ship and Anchor tell stories about them. They didn't speak Caerda and did all sorts of strange things.

The woman walked forward and bent down, bringing up a wide pot with a handle. With it she scooped up water and tossed it at Jin.

"Hey!" It was cold enough to make him gasp, and then he realized the burning feeling wasn't as bad. When she was finished, the girl handed him a bowl with something white in it. Jin drank. The white liquid was thick and tart and the best thing he'd ever had. He drained the bowl completely.

"Thanks." Jin handed back the bowl, wondering if he could get more. "Where is this place?"

"This is Gilbadeh, the nearest village to the fort." The girl gave him a suspicious look. "How can you not be of the fort? You are pale like them, and you speak the language they use."

"*You're* using it," Jin pointed out. "Everybody speaks it where I come from."

"It is very strange—but even the fort people know not to go out in the hottest part of the day. Or to try to get inside a *kanah*."

"Kaa naah?"

The girl shrugged. "The square towers. They let the air go through and cool our homes. Some of the workers heard strange noises during their rest and went to see, and found you near death from the sun."

The woman spoke again. Her voice had a gentle, calm quality that made Jin wonder if she was one of the genteel, or what passed for such in this place. He could see thin, gold bracelets on her wrists, too. If she was genteel, why was she taking care of him? Genteel folk in Thama didn't take notice of street boys like Jin, even if they were dying.

"My mother will put medicine on you now," the girl said.

"Um, what am I to call you, please?" Genteel folk were always fussing about manners, and he didn't want to offend. Mr. Andel was genteel, or he had been once, anyway. He was always polite, even to the street folk. He'd want Jin to be polite to people who were helping him, and speak well, even if they were foreigners. *No one is so poor they cannot afford courtesy*, he'd say.

The girl hesitated, glancing at her mother. "I am Zinde."

"I'm Jin." Both women gasped and drew back, Zinde's mother drawing the thin cloth covering her face more tightly with one hand. "What's wrong?" Jin felt a wave of dizziness. The cool water had dried on his skin, and he was feeling hot and sick again.

Zinde's mother sighed and shook her head. She bent and lifted up a wicker basket from the stream, and from it took a clay jar. She knelt beside Jin's bed and gestured for him to lower the sheet he was clutching to his chest. Jin hesitated, unsure, and she opened the jar to show him a thick green paste. It smelled of herbs, sharp and clean.

"It will help the sun sickness," Zinde said.

Jin reluctantly lowered his hands. Zinde's mother ruffled his hair softly with one hand, her eyes crinkling in what might have been a smile, if he could see her face. The green paste was cold and stung a little when it first went on, but then his burning skin went numb. He almost sobbed in relief as the pain faded away.

Zinde crouched down beside her mother, giving Jin a suspicious look. "Is that really your name?" Jin nodded. "*Za.* You do not look like it. In our tongue, *janh* means...I am not sure how to say. Deposit? No!" Her eyes brightened. "I remember now. *Demon.*"

CHAPTER 4
THE PEOPLE OF THE FORT

Jin noticed with surprise that he didn't need to pour water on himself anymore, and the light from the lamp didn't hurt his eyes like it had at first. He thought about it and realized it had been at least a week since he had first woken up in the water tunnel. He scratched his shoulder absently, feeling the dry skin peel off. He was shedding skin like a snake. Maybe that was why he was so hungry.

He was getting stronger, too—strong enough to walk a little. He had explored the entire space he was in as soon as he could stand—Zinde called it the water tunnel. The water flowed in from darkness, through an even smaller tunnel, and out the same way. The water channel was against the wall of the tunnel, and a broad stone shelf extended on the other side to a wall of stone blocks. The wall had a sturdy wooden door—but made of wood bars to let the air through—which led to the rest of the house. Zinde and her mother kept food cool by leaving it in the water in floating gourds, anchored by strings to the wall.

The familiar shifting flicker of lamplight angled down through the door, and he gathered the sheet up around him.

"*Wasa,* Jinli." Zinde stepped through the door with a bowl in one hand and a chain with a lamp at the end in the other. She hung the lamp from a hook and adjusted the thin scarf over her face.

"*Wasa*, Zinde." Jin looked hopefully at the bowl. It was covered with a piece of the strange bread they ate here, like a flapjack but chewy. He was starting to like it.

He was learning some of their foreign talk, too, like how to say hello. They called their language Rabani, which also seemed to be the name of the country. When Jin asked them what direction Caerdon was from Rabani, they looked at him like he was raving.

Zinde and her mother, Une Karestal, had taken to calling him Jinli. Zinde told him a *jinli* was a kind of small cake. They liked that name better than his real one, and Jin didn't mind. For all their strangeness, they had taken care of him when he was sick and fed him better than he had been fed in months. Longer, even. Since Mr. Andel died.

Zinde sat down gracefully beside the mat. She made the motion look like she was floating, and she could stand up the same way. Jin could not figure out how she did it.

"I must speak with you," she said in a low tone as she glanced over her shoulder at the door, handing him the bowl.

Jin nodded while stuffing his face with the food. Usually Une Karestal was there too when Zinde came, but it looked like Zinde wanted to tell him something in secret. Zinde had her eyes locked on her hands, wrapped around her knees, and that was strange, too. Usually she just stared at him with a hard expression.

"We don't have enough food," she said bluntly. Jin

froze, a piece of the flat bread in his fingers. "Mother says you are growing and it is wrong to keep food from you, but now she is hungry and I say that is wrong, too. And she won't eat my share, either."

Jin attempted to speak, but a crumb went down the wrong way and he coughed. "I'm not sick anymore," he said when he stopped coughing. "I can leave."

Zinde shook her head. "You must stay hidden. The *maahtik* would see you." That was another word he had learned. The people of the fort, the *maaht*. "The council has been arguing what to do. They fear the *maahtik* will be angry, thinking we stole you. And when they are angry, my people die." Her eyes blazed over her thin scarf. "We are afraid of everything. Even your clothes we have washed at night, so their strangeness is not seen."

His clothes! "I had some things I found, in the pockets. Maybe you could sell those...but I guess those would look strange, too," he said, remembering the iron locks. "Did you...there was a little round thing..." Jin really didn't want to give it up, but it was the only thing of value he had, and a debt was a debt.

Zinde reached into the colorful sash at her waist and pulled out the crystal sphere. It flared in the lamplight, casting fiery reflections on the wall of the water tunnel. Jin reached for it instinctively, then forced his hands back.

"You can have it." It was hard to say. But he needed to eat. It was stupid to keep something just because it was pretty.

Zinde made an exasperated sound and tossed both hands in the air, making her bracelets jangle. "Do you not listen? The *maahtik* would kill everyone in the village if they saw this!"

Jin sat up straight, excited. "Do you know what it is?"

"No. But I know the *maahtik* have several such things they keep guarded as the greatest treasure," she said, turning the sphere in the light and examining it closely.

"How do you know, if they hide them?" Jin asked.

Her dark eyes narrowed, and she ducked her head. "I was hiding, too," she whispered. "I was trying to find my father. He works there, but he hasn't been seen for months. The *maahtik* say he died in an explosion in the mine, that his body is gone. I think they are lying." Her eyes blazed. "He had no reason to go to the mine, and no one heard any explosion. But no one has seen him inside the *maaht*, either. I heard the *maahtik* speak of a prisoner when they did not know I could hear. I think...I think he is that prisoner."

"Why would they put him in prison?"

Zinde shrugged, wrapping her arms around her knees again and resting her head there, too. "Who knows why they do anything? It is of no importance. I must find and free him. If you will help me, I will give this back to you."

"How can I help if you don't want them to see me?" Jin couldn't keep his eyes from the crystal sphere between her fingers. It was strange how he wanted it so bad, and it frightened him a little.

"You and the *maahtik* come from the same place. You look as they do; you speak their language. What my people fear is your being found with us. If you are only seen inside the *maaht*, how can they blame us? And there is another reason." Zinde bent closer and whispered, "No one knows how the *maahtik* came here. They first appeared in my great-grandfather's time, as if they had dropped from the sky. They were not like the *maahtik* now," she said slowly. "The *maaht* had not been built then, and they would trade with us. But no one had ever heard of their land named Caerdon, and they did not know the names of any country in Darha."

"Is that how you know my language?"

Zinde nodded. "My father learned it to work in the *maaht*, and he taught me so I might find work there, too. He once told me, new people appear inside the *maaht* without any traveler being seen outside. They work magic—this is known. A beast of metal fed with coal serves them in the mines. Perhaps there is a magic door to their world in the *maaht*—and you can return."

Jin blinked. He'd fallen through the hole that had appeared in midair, in the warehouse, and found himself in this world. A door...a door between worlds. But it hadn't been there before, and he'd never heard anyone speak of such a thing. Why had it appeared for him?

The crystal sphere. The door appeared when he held the sphere. But no door opened when Zinde held it. And he'd held it when he stood in the hot sand, and nothing had happened then, either. Maybe it only worked once.

Zinde tilted her head, glancing at him from the corners of her eyes. "Will you do it?"

"Why can't you? People notice when someone new shows up, and I would have to be seen to get inside." Jin had developed useful experience in his short career of "finding" things.

"I only work there a few days every month, when they need extra hands. I can't go when I wish, or I would be there every day. That is the only money we have to live on, since my father is missing—and it isn't enough."

Jin scowled at her. "So you are going to risk that? Get yourself and the village in trouble just to look around? You'll be even hungrier if you have no money at all."

Zinde lunged forward, now on her knees, confronting Jin mere inches away. Her eyes blazed. "For my father I would die a thousand deaths! If it was your father, would you not do the same?"

Jin hunched and looked away. "Dunno. Seems to me you have to do for yourself if nobody does for you."

Her eyes widened, and her shoulders sagged. "But...Jinli! Your family. Don't you care about them?"

"Don't have any. Never did." Jin knew about family, in theory. The people he knew in Thama had family, sometimes. If death hadn't taken them, or the billies. Mr. Andel had tried to explain everyone had a father and a mother, even if they might not be there anymore, but to Jin, family was something that happened to other people.

"No...no home? Where did you live?"

He snorted. "The old stable on Highwater Street. Had a hidey-hole the stable hands didn't know about, in the hayloft, but that all burned down in the fire. I got nothing now."

His first memories were of Mrs. Keters and the big kitchen of the carter's inn. There was always something for a small boy to do there, and he was paid in kitchen scraps. She was a rough and violent woman, overfond of drink, but she had taken a small interest in him and given him much-patched clothes and his precious blanket. Then Mrs. Keters got the coughing sickness and the inn owner wanted another boy in the kitchen, and he'd had to find other work. Mostly hanging about the Ship and Anchor and running errands for a penny, which was how he had met Mr. Andel. Mr. Andel had frequently been too ill to leave his bed and would send out for food to the inn.

Thinking about it, Jin supposed he would have done an awful lot to help Mr. Andel. Did do, in the end. Nobody else seemed to care what happened to him. And Jin was good at finding things that nobody else wanted.

Then he noticed Zinde hadn't said anything for a while, and looked up. She had drawn the thin scarf over her entire face, covering even her eyes, and her head hung down. Slowly one hand extended toward Jin, holding out the crystal sphere. He hesitated, confused, then took it. It felt warm and comforting in his hand. Like it belonged there.

"Why? I haven't even done anything. I thought you wanted me to help find your father."

Zinde sniffled, head down. *"Bis'adah tak haraki."*

Jin sighed. "I don't know those words. What are they in Caerda?"

"My heart weeps blood for my father, and I will not know rest until I find him. But he would spurn me if he knew I was *haraki*. The words mean 'one who takes from the hopeless.' It is the worst thing that can be said of anyone, among my people. I am not *haraki!*" Her voice was rough and tight, like she was trying not to cry.

"I didn't...I want to help you. I just don't see how I can."

Zinde looked up, and this time he could see her eyes. But before she could speak, Jin heard another voice calling her.

"*Jah, Une!*" Zinde said. She bent toward Jin quickly and whispered, "Hide it! Don't let anyone see!"

And then Une Karestal was opening the door, holding his clean and patched clothing in her arms. She spoke, and Zinde's eyes widened in surprise.

"She says to dress yourself. The elders wish to speak with you when the sun has set."

CHAPTER 5
A MATTER OF VILLAGE-HONOR

Jin was worried but still eager to finally leave the water tunnel. And it felt very good to be wearing his clothes again instead of just a sheet. He felt weak and a little dizzy, but that got better as he walked more.

Une Karestal led him through the slatted wood door, and he saw their home for the first time. It was very bare and, like the water tunnel, was carved from the rock, a pale gold sandy stone. A few wood chests, some hangings on the wall, and rugs and pillows and a low table in one corner made up the furnishings. Dark arches probably led to the other rooms.

Beyond the main room was a sloping ramp that curved to one side and widened at the top. The air got warmer as they ascended. A large, carved door with a heavy, complicated wooden latch was directly in front of him, and to either side were pegs with long, dark fabric hanging from them.

Une Karestal took down one length of fabric and swirled it around Jin. A light frame that looked like a hat mold made of wicker was placed on his head, and the dark fabric came over it and down to his feet. He was completely covered and hidden, and his unusual clothes, too.

He looked over at Zinde and stumbled back against the wall, startled. Where she had been was one of the dark towers of his dream. Only now he could see she was also wearing one of the robes with the hat frame, just like he was. The towers had been people, then. The people who had heard and rescued him.

"Cover your face," Zinde said. "You must pretend to be one of us, and our people do not show themselves openly as the *maahtik* do."

Puzzled, Jin pulled the fabric lower over the frame, in front of his face. How would he see? Then he realized the fabric was light and loosely woven, and the lamplight was visible through it. He could even make out the dark shapes of Zinde and Une Karestal.

Une Karestal opened the big door, and Zinde followed, carrying the lamp. Outside, the sky was dark, with deep purple and rose from the sunset still visible. The air was dry and dusty, still carrying the heat of the day. It was much warmer than inside the house. Looking back, Jin saw the door to the house was set in the rock face of a crumbling cliff. Farther down he could see other doors, some with metal lamps hanging next to them, with small, flickering flames inside.

One of the lamps looked like the winged creature he had seen in the sand, with cuts in the metal that made the light glow just like the red lines on the creature's skin. He blinked, surprised. It must be real —not something he'd imagined when he'd had the sun sickness. He wanted to ask Zinde about the creature but stopped in time. Speaking the language of the fort people would be just as bad as showing his clothes.

Nobody else seemed to be outside. He heard a howling cry in the distance, and wind tugged at the black fabric of his robe as they walked. Eventually they came to an empty square, set with flat stones.

The cliff was lower here, and a real building had been constructed facing the square. It had double doors, with torches on either side, and two guards in front.

The men did not speak as Jin and the others approached, but silently opened the doors. They were not wearing the enveloping black robes, but they did have the scarves that wrapped over their heads and covered the lower parts of their faces. The skin around their eyes was a darker brown than Zinde's or Une Karestal's. They carried thick wood staffs and wore leather armor over white tunics and baggy trousers. Jin wondered why the guards didn't have guns, or even swords.

Inside, a large crowd was seated on the ground and talking excitedly. Many small glass lamps hung from the beams of the room, and larger metal lamps stood on tables in the corners. One end of the room had a raised platform, covered with rugs and a kind of cushioned bench. Five older men sat there, one gently waving a flat, white thing pierced with holesback and forth before his face. A fan?

As soon as Jin and the two women entered, the talking stopped. Everyone who didn't have their scarves over their faces drew them across as soon as they saw him, but the old men left their faces uncovered. The one with the white fan beckoned, and Zinde nudged Jin's shoulder. Reluctantly, he stepped forward. He could feel everyone watching him. He'd always tried to stay out of sight, to stay out of trouble, to not be noticed. Were they mad at him? He didn't *mean* to do anything wrong, but sometimes he did anyway.

The old men didn't look too happy. Maybe they didn't like him wearing the hat thing. You were supposed to take your hat off to show respect to the genteel and billies and the like. Jin hadn't owned a hat for a long time and had forgotten. He awkwardly lifted the hat frame off.

That seemed to startle them, and everybody else in the room, judging by the whispers and gasps. One of the old men leaned forward and peered at him, as if he couldn't believe what he was seeing.

"You *maahtik?*" he said, in a high, creaky voice. It sounded different than when Zinde spoke, and harder to understand.

"Um, I didn't come from the fort, sir." Jin gripped the hat frame tighter in his hands. "I come from Thama, I guess."

Jin heard someone walk up beside him. Zinde. She spoke in Rabani. The old men listened to her, then looked at Jin again before one asked another question. This time she translated.

"They want to know how you came here, and for what purpose."

Jin told the whole story, only leaving out the crystal sphere, which was now carefully hidden in the lining of his coat. "...and I didn't know I would come here. I just wanted to get warm," he finished, looking down at his bare feet. "I'm sorry I made trouble for you. I'd go back, but I don't know how."

The old men talked in whispers among themselves, then asked another question.

"What do you know of the *maaht?*"

Jin shrugged, puzzled. "I never been in it. I never even *seen* it, I don't think." Then he remembered being out in the sand, and something tall and brownish in the distance. Maybe that was the fort?

More argument from the crowd. People sounded

angry. Jin glanced about, wondering what to do. Could he run? Where would he run to? He was starting to feel dizzy and weak, too. He hadn't recovered completely from being sick.

"They can't decide if you are a spy or not," Zinde whispered. "It is good we did not tell them your real name."

Jin nodded and staggered when he lost his balance. The old man with the fan regarded him for a moment, not unkindly.

"You go, sleep. We talk, say tomorrow." He gestured with the fan toward the door.

"Um, pardon, sir." Jin shifted on his feet, staggering again. "I don't got any call on you, but maybe you know of work I could do...least enough to earn my meals?"

Zinde gave him a warm look as she translated, the ends of her eyes turning up. He could just see a smile under her dark scarf.

The crowd sounded less unhappy now. One large man stood and spoke, gesturing at Jin. He had very dark eyes, completely black and with a hard expression in them. Whatever he said, Zinde did not like. She whirled to face him, her scarf flying about. Her response was angry and quick, and Jin heard the word she had said before—*haraki*. She was pointing to the large man when she said it. Then she turned back to the older men, speaking in a torrent of words, her hands gesturing to them, the entire crowd, and then Jin.

The elder with the white fan held up a hand for quiet, then spoke. A quiet voice answered from the back—Une Karestal. The crowd listened in silence, lowering their eyes and not looking at Jin. A soft murmur filled the room.

Jin eyed Zinde. "What did you say?"

Her eyes narrowed. "I told them what you said, that you had nothing and no kin. He *said* he would feed you, but everyone knows he is mean and grasping. It would be very little, if he ever did pay you. I warned them of the insult to village-honor if we were *haraki*, that is all. Une told them of your thinness and the many old scars you bear, proving you are poor."

The elder gestured for silence and spoke again, his rising tone indicating a question this time.

Then another man stood. He was short but burly, strong muscles visible under his robes, and hands like slabs. One arm was in a sling. He simply said, "*Za.*"

This seemed to please the elders, and the crowd had a general air of relief.

"What is it?" Jin whispered to Zinde.

"Hasnen a'Kanahti has agreed to give you work, and will pay you as well as give you meals. It is well thought, and it will help him until his arm heals." Jin saw the flash of a white grin under her scarf. "And the *maahtik* will not see you! He is our well digger."

CHAPTER 6
MORO

Jin left with Hasnen a'Kanahti that night. Zinde frowned when this was announced, and had a great deal to say to Hasnen. He listened patiently, his dark eyes revealing nothing, until Une Karestal finally came up to take Zinde by the hand and pull her away.

"I told him you do not speak much Rabani," she called over her shoulder. "You are still to rest for a while—I will come and teach you more words!"

Hasnen watched her go, then turned to Jin. Faint crinkles of amusement deepened around his eyes for a moment, then he pointed to the pile of black cloth and then Jin. "*Kebba*," he said.

Jin struggled with the wicker frame and the fabric, trying to remember how Une Karestal had done it. He ended up with a tangled mess, but Hasnen seemed to think it would be enough and headed for the door.

Following Hasnen's broad, sturdy back out into the night, Jin hoped they would not have to walk too far. They passed the courtyard and a few low buildings and started up a path steep enough Jin had to stop and catch his breath more than once. The path leveled out and broadened, with a cliff face on one side and a dark valley below. Hasnen turned at the far end, at a large door with a simple lantern hanging beside it.

When the door opened, a boy jumped up from a

low, cushioned bench, asking a question that abruptly stopped when he caught sight of Jin. Hasnen said a few words, gesturing at his injured arm and then at Jin before taking a wooden bar and placing it in two brackets across the door.

Jin was tired of the black thing—the *kebba?*—and he pulled it off, thrashing his arms and flailing. The boy laughed, then gasped. When Jin was able to see, he was staring at Jin, his eyes wide. He was a little older than Jin, or at least taller, and had the same kind of sturdy build as Hasnen.

Hasnen gestured, frowning. "*Tak, Moro. Iye noori.*"

The boy's face reddened. Then he grinned at Jin and darted through the cloth-hung doorway on the far wall, returning with a shallow wooden platter full of the flat bread things and a chipped ceramic pot. The pot was full of soft, tart cheese, which they scooped up using torn-off pieces of flat bread, spreading the cheese on the rest of the bread. It was simple food, but filling.

The boy poured from a jug into a small pottery bowl and handed it to Jin. Then he pointed to himself. "Moro."

Jin sipped from the bowl. It was some kind of cold tea, tasting slightly of apples. "Jin—Jinli," he said, remembering just in time to use his nickname.

"Jinli a'Tema," added Hasnen. Jin puzzled about that for a moment, then realized he was trying to say Thama. So when Zinde had spoken of Hasnen a'Kanahti, and *kanah* were the towers for water cooling, it was just saying what he was—the one who dug for that water.

Hasnen and Moro talked for some time, or rather Moro talked a lot, and his father spoke briefly. Jin knew they were talking about him, but nothing more than that.

A soft tap, repeated, came from the door. Hasnen looked up sharply, pointing at Jin and then at the curtained archway in back. Moro jumped to his feet and pulled Jin up, dragging him behind the curtain.

Jin heard the bar lifted and the door opened, and Hasnen speaking softly. Then the door closed, followed by the bar dropping back in place. Huddled against the wall with Moro, Jin could feel him relax.

"Jah, Moro."

That seemed to be the signal to come out again. With the curtain pulled back, Jin saw Hasnen was holding a small pile of clothing, which he handed to Jin. It was the same kind of thing the villagers wore, loose cloth trousers that came just below the knee and a tunic with long sleeves, all in a dust-brown color.

Moro patted the cushioned bench, tilting his head and closing his eyes, then opening them and looking at Jin. Time to sleep. Jin was exhausted and glad to follow the suggestion.

Breakfast the next day was a bowl of boiled grain with some ground meat mixed in. The door was unbarred and Hasnen had already gone. Moro tried to explain, but Jin couldn't figure out what all the gestures were trying to describe. Giving up, Moro handed Jin a broom. This he had no difficulty understanding.

Jin swept up, and then Moro showed him the stable. Their house was built underground, similar to Zinde's, except that it looked like a big cave had been dug first and then a house built inside it. Next to that was an open space where the donkey was kept. First

Moro had to close the rough wood doors to the stable, and then with pointing and waving the black cloth—the *kebba*—around, tell Jin he couldn't go outside or be seen from outside unless he was wearing it.

The two of them cleaned out the stable, Jin shoveling and Moro taking the manure outside in a wheelbarrow. Jin managed to finish before having to stop and rest. He was getting stronger, and he didn't feel dizzy anymore.

Then Moro showed him how to refill the water barrel. "*Kahnati!*" he said, grinning and pointing down the dark hole at the back of the stable. A long, round piece of wood was suspended over it, and a rope hung down into the darkness.

Moro started to turn the handle at the end of the round piece of wood, and the rope wound itself around it. Slowly, a wooden bucket full of water rose up at the end of the rope. Jerking his head at it, Moro indicated Jin was to take the bucket and empty it in the barrel.

By the time the barrel was full, Jin was exhausted again, and the sun was hot. Moro led him through the back of the house, showing him the soot-grimed kitchen and a familiar-looking slatted door that led to their water tunnel. It was larger than the one at Zinde's house, and Jin could see where the hole was that went to the stable. The water channel was wider and deeper, too.

Moro picked up the cooling jug of tea from the water, and collecting some flat bread, they sat down to eat. It was too hot to do much, and Jin was still very tired, so Moro showed him how to play a game with white and black pebbles, tossing them so they landed in circles or close to, but not touching, the other player's pebbles.

"*Iye Moro a'Khanati, beza lalil otorok!*" came a familiar voice from outside.

Moro looked up, grinning. "*Iye Zinde a'Karestal, azazi panir!*" He got to his feet and opened the door, loosely winding a scarf about his face.

Zinde came in, swathed in her *kebba*. She removed it in a single swirling motion that Jin hoped he could remember next time he had to take his off.

"*Wasa*, Jinli! It is good to see this clumsy one has not dropped you in a well." She held out a black pot, covered with a cloth that was tied at the neck with a string. "Une sends this for your sun sickness."

A familiar scent of pungent herbs came from the pot. "I'm almost all better. Only a little red in places, and it doesn't hurt anymore." Jin clutched the pot and felt strangely happy, seeing the medicine. Une Karestal still thought about him, even if he wasn't in her house anymore. What were the words Mr. Andel had said, when someone did him a kindness? "Please tell her I am...much obliged."

Moro had gone and returned with a bowl for Zinde, who had seated herself on a threadbare cushion. She drank the cold tea in gulps, wiping her face under her scarf. "Uff! Une said I could come here, but only at the height of the sun when the *maahtik* are not about—and I may only leave when it is dark."

"That's good. Moro keeps trying to tell me things and I don't understand him."

Zinde sat up, her eyes bright. "I will help you. What do you want to learn?"

Jin spread his hands. "Everything! What did you

say before you came in?" Moro had laughed, and Jin wanted to know what the joke was.

Zinde repeated the words in Rabani, a glint of mischief in her eyes. "In your tongue, I would say... 'See Moro, the hunter of chickens!' When he was very young, he would chase chickens—and cry when he could not catch them. We greet those we know well in this way."

Moro said something, grinning so broadly the corner of his mouth was visible over the scarf. Zinde made an outraged noise and threw one of the smaller cushions at him, which just made Moro laugh even harder, sputtering as he spoke.

"What is it?"

She didn't say anything for a moment, her brows knotted over a stormy gaze. Then she lifted her chin. "He says I should tell you what *he* said. If I don't, he will wait until you know the words and tell you himself, so it doesn't matter. His words were 'See Zinde, killer of bread!' When Une first taught me to cook, I would always burn the bread," she said in a small voice. "But I do it better now!"

"*Za, za,*" Moro said soothingly, holding up his hands.

Jin mumbled the words to himself, repeating the meaning in his mind. Then what Zinde had just said reminded him of a question he'd had for a while.

"Do the people here always use first names when they talk about someone? You say Une all the time, and that's what she said to me, too. But...for us it's not manners, at least for me to speak to someone older."

"Une is not her name!" Zinde giggled. "It means mother. And *aba* means father."

Jin blinked. "Won't she be angry if I call her Mother?"

She shook her head. "That is how we speak here. It doesn't mean she's *your* mother. Now, what else do you need words for?"

For the rest of the hot afternoon Zinde translated and explained, with frequent interruptions by Moro, who had many questions for Jin. Jin learned he wasn't going to be digging new wells so much as keeping the existing ones cleared out. Hasnen was out at a neighboring village that wanted a *kanah* built for them, marking where the vertical shafts would go. Someone else would dig them, since he could not until his arm healed. Then he would dig the horizontal tunnel that actually carried the water, a much more difficult task.

Moro wanted to know how old he was, and if everyone in Caerda had white skin and pale eyes, and what games Jin played there. Jin didn't know his age, which puzzled them. Neither Moro nor Zinde believed Jin when he told them some people had hair red as fire, or gold. Moro found some pieces of reed so Jin could show them how to play peg-string, but his face fell when Jin described keep-away-stray, the other game Jin liked that involved several players.

"Moro does not often have the chance to see others our age," Zinde explained. "When his mother was alive, and he was young, she would come and visit Une and bring him, but now he must help his father." Moro mumbled something, and she added, "he does not like working underground, especially by himself. He is glad you are here now and promises to lower you and bring you up with the winding-crank so you do not have to climb the rope."

Jin brightened. He had not been looking forward to lots of digging, so this was good news. "I *like* climbing."

CHAPTER 7
HELPING ZINDE

"Jah, a'Tama!"

Something blocked the light from the well shaft, and Jin looked up. The round, cheerful face of Moro a'Kanahti was visible at the top.

"I hear noise; it is wind!" he yelled back.

Moro grinned. "Bah, hear the demon try to speak as a man! Come up. Zinde has brought fruit and news. It is safe—no one else is in sight, and I have your *kebba* here."

Jin felt a surprising burst of happiness. He had not seen Zinde for nearly a week, since he had been out clearing wells for a distant village. He was learning the language very quickly, but it was still easier to speak with her than try to figure out all the strange new words by himself.

He had been working for the well digger for over a month. He had learned how to climb down the access shafts of the existing *kanah* to clear out mud and fallen rock. The shafts went straight down and connected to the tunnels that carried the water. It was hard work, but it was out of the sun. Jin was the perfect height to walk in the tunnels, which were just as high as his head. Moro and his father had to bend over to fit.

Sometimes he had to carry a lamp in the dark tunnels, if the blockage was far from the shaft. Moro hated working underground in the dark, so he had been very happy to let Jin take over that task. Instead, Moro cranked up the baskets of mud and dumped them out as fast as Jin could fill them. They were heavy, but Moro was quite strong for his size.

Jin could see the red color of sunset in the little spot of sky at the top of the shaft. Time to stop work anyway. Jin gathered up his tools and put them in the empty basket tied to the end of the rope, then washed the mud off as best he could.

He put his hand on the climbing rope. "Start pulling!"

The basket lurched up as Jin jumped and climbed. Before Moro pulled it completely out, Jin had put his hand on the top of the brick wall surrounding the shaft entrance.

"Ah, bah! Not again!" Moro tossed the black cloth of the *kebba* around Jin as he climbed out, and shoved the wicker frame at him. "This one is the deepest yet! I was sure I would beat you this time."

"I win. I climb faster than he pulls up tools," Jin explained to Zinde. He was panting a little, but not as much as he used to when he first started. Moro didn't even try to beat him climbing the rope anymore.

They were on the headlands north of Gilbadeh, in the hills. A few trees and shrubs grew here, but they were sparse and offered little shade. Jin, Zinde, and Moro crouched in the shadow of the brick wall instead, draping the edges of their *kebba* over sticks planted in the ground for more air.

"The first of the harvest," Zinde said, uncovering the basket under her *kebba*. It held small, purple-red fruit with a rich, deep scent and tart juice. Jin ate handfuls, spitting out the seeds and wondering how he could still be thirsty when he worked all day standing knee-deep in water.

"Why build wall around hole?" Jin licked sticky juice off his fingers, struggling for the right words in Rabani. "Harder to get out."

"It also keeps out sand," Moro said, reaching for the last of the fruit. "And goats. You have been fortunate. You have not had to remove any dead animals yet." He grinned.

Zinde made the gesture meant to avert bad luck.

"Is Une Karestal well?" Jin asked. "I have first pay. Night, I get and give you."

Zinde glared, and Moro groaned and rolled his eyes.

"See Jinli a'Tema, an outsider of great rudeness. It is good you only say this where we hear. Why do you wish to insult this good woman? You owe her much."

"Yes, yes! But how I pay debt? You need money. Strange people..."

Zinde sighed. "It is insulting to repay hospitality with money, as if it were a thing bought in the market." She glanced at Jin and spoke in Caerda. "It is...for a debt of this kind, you...you give a gift. *Not* money."

"Oh." It was all very confusing. Jin still didn't understand all the customs, like the face scarf. It was important who you showed your face to, that much he had figured out. But not why. Moro did not cover his face for Jin, but did tuck his scarf up a little when Zinde was present, or strangers from another village. Zinde always kept her scarf up. "Would you...what gift would she like? What should I do?"

"What we spoke of before." Zinde held her thumb and forefinger apart, the width of the crystal sphere, and gave him a meaningful look. Then she switched back to Rabani. "You have not asked me my news. It is just now announced. The festival will be in three days. The *maaht* festival," she added.

Jin blinked, suddenly understanding. "Oh. You work then. Good." With a sinking feeling he remembered she planned to get him inside as well.

Zinde nodded vigorously, dislodging her scarf. "They always need more who speak their tongue to serve them then." She tucked her scarf back up.

Moro sat up, frowning. "Jinli can't...the elders would not permit it! Even if he didn't look like he was made of cheese, he has water-eyes just like the *maahtik* do!"

Zinde widened her eyes. "Of course not! What, did you think I would suggest he be hired too? That would be foolish." For a moment, her voice sounded like Thumbless Bode trying to convince a billy he was an honest citizen.

"Yes, it would be foolish." Moro narrowed his eyes at her. "And you are known for doing foolish things, when you do not take the time to think. It would be best if you did not go to the *maaht* at all."

"I have no choice." It sounded like Zinde was speaking between gritted teeth.

Moro dropped his head. "I know this," he said softly. "Remember that your danger is danger to your friends as well. Do not ask Jinli to help you with your tricks."

"You may go dig a hole and sit in it," she snapped. Then she tilted her head at Moro, looking up at him. "Don't worry, ancient father. They have me carrying water and running everywhere during the day, and at night all the servers are shut up in the kitchen and can't get out. I give you my honor-word, I will not leave the kitchen unless someone unbars the door—and the guards do not do that until dawn."

Moro grunted and ate the last few berries thoughtfully. "Last festival, the *maahtik* were everywhere in the village making their arrangements. The *kanah* we work on now ends nearby. It will be too dangerous for you to work there, Jinli. Even the *maahtik* know we do not work in *kebba*, and they would notice you."

"He can stay in your house, then, until the festival ends."

Moro shook his head. "Better if he is nowhere near the village. I think he should hide in the caves near the mines. My father and I can take him there tomorrow." Jin felt a rush of relief. It wasn't that he didn't want to help Zinde, but her idea was sounding more and more dangerous.

"But—" Zinde hesitated, then said brightly, "yes, that is a good idea! You should do that." She stood and stretched, bending down again for the basket. "Oh, is that your father already?" When Moro jumped up and scanned the horizon, she whispered in Jin's ear, "At one hand of moon, go to the small-need!"

Jin could see the small cart coming down the hills where Hasnen a'Kanahti had been working. Zinde waved to the cart, then to them as she walked back to the village.

One hand of moon meant when the moon was one hand's width above the horizon, and the small-need was their term for the outhouse. Jin worried about what to do the whole time he was waiting. He could get there without too much trouble. It was easy to pretend to be tired after the simple meal with Hasnen and Moro—Une Karestal was a much better cook—and then at the appointed time step out as if he were just going to the small-need for its intended purpose.

He finally decided he had to go. Maybe he could think of another way to help her, or get her to change her mind.

When he reached the small-need, Zinde was already there, a pool of deep black in the shadows.

"We must get you inside the *maaht*, Jinli," she said softly. "There is not much time. In two days I go and will not return until the festival is done."

Jin had seen the fort at a distance. It looked impossible to break in to. It was guarded, too, and not by villagers. He thought about how he had gotten inside places in Thama.

"Do they use the *kanah* for water? I am small enough to go all the way through the tunnels."

She shook her head. "If they do, a'Kanahti did not dig it for them."

"And he won't dig it for you, either."

Zinde jumped, making a startled squeak. Jin was ready to run but then realized it was Moro that had spoken.

"See Zinde a'Karestal, foolish girl by her own words! Do we not have enough trouble with the *maahtik*, that you seek more?" Moro sounded furious. "Why are you trying to bring Jinli to the *maaht?* Did you not give your honor-word to me?"

"I said I would stay in the kitchen until the door was unbarred, and I will! Jinli will let me out. How did you know I was here?" Zinde said. "Go back to sleep!"

"Jinli does not know you are a fountain of trouble, but I do. I suspected you were plotting something and followed him. Why, Zinde? What is worth this?"

Zinde drew a curved, shining blade from under her robe. "Blood. My heart says my father lives, as a prisoner. I will see my father or avenge his death."

Moro froze. "You have...they search all who go inside. And weapons are forbidden us anywhere."

"They are not forbidden to Jinli, because he is from the world of the *maahtik*. I brought the sword for him to hide. If he can get within the *maaht*, bringing this with him is a small matter."

"If I get in," Jin said, feeling uncomfortable. He'd never used a sword. It wasn't exactly illegal to have a knife in Thama, but stabbing anyone would get the billies on you faster than stealing.

Moro turned on him. "And why do you do this? They could kill you, even if they are your people."

Jin shrugged. "I owe Zinde a debt. And if they catch me, the village will not be blamed." It didn't sound like much of a reason when he said it, but Moro nodded his head slowly.

"I see. I will help you."

"Why?" Zinde sounded suspicious, and Jin couldn't blame her.

"You must go and work, so you and your mother will have food. You will do something foolish no matter what I say. Better Jinli and I help you, if we cannot stop you." Moro sighed. "And the *maahtik* owe blood to more than you. It is village-honor. It is still a stupid plan, but not as stupid as your plans usually are. With Jinli, we have a chance. And I know how he can get inside without being seen." He clapped Jinli on the shoulder, his grin a flash of white in the darkness. "All you must do is find enough rope when you are inside, and take it to the roof."

CHAPTER 8
HARVEST FESTIVAL

The cave Moro found for Jin was high in the hills over the village of Gilbadeh. Jin could see everything from the cave entrance—the village, the fort, and even trees and fields of the deepest part of the valley. He had wondered why the village wasn't in the valley instead, but Moro had explained the farmland was so valuable it would be a waste to put a house on it.

Today was the day of the festival, and after two days in hiding Jin was quite ready to leave. He had already explored his cave, which hadn't taken long because it wasn't very deep. Then he had investigated the area nearby, always being careful to wear his sand-colored Rabani clothing to blend in so he could not be seen easily. He was curious about the *maahtik*'s mine and the strange noises he heard, and searched until he found a little tunnel formed by two giant boulders wedged against each other. It was just big enough for him to wiggle through, and one end overlooked the mine entrance. That kept him occupied the rest of the time.

He had to wait until the sun was fully set before leaving, and it would be several hours. Jin decided to go look at the mine again. As he got closer to the boulders, he could tell something was different. The chuffing, thumping noise he sometimes heard faintly was quite loud—and when he scrambled to the edge and looked down, he saw why.

A huge mechanical device was sitting just outside the mine entrance, black smoke gushing from a pipe in the back. It was sitting on the metal rails that had puzzled Jin earlier, and what looked like a claw on a jointed arm extended from the front. People were working on the device and yelling to each other over the noise it made.

Jin had heard of steam locomotives but had never seen one. He didn't think this was a locomotive, even though it did move on rails. Sometimes people pushed carts full of rubble out of the mine on those rails and dumped them down the hillside.

Someone shouted, and a big belch of smoke came from the rumbling machine—and the arm with the claw extended. Jin drew a sharp breath. It was almost like the machine was alive! The arm didn't go all the way, though, and that made the people shout more.

He watched as the sun started to go down. After a great deal of work, the claw-arm moved all the way, and the whole machine slowly moved back into the mine. A string of workers, all chained together, came out of the mine with their picks and shovels. They were grimy and thin, drooping with exhaustion. Other workers, crowded in simple three-sided sheds, were being gathered up to go to work in their place—all except for one, who had not gotten up when the others had. The man in charge pointed, and two workers went to pick up the one on the ground and put him in a cart, then pushed it to the hillside.

It made Jin very uncomfortable when he understood. The man in the cart was dead, and they weren't even going to bury him—just dump him over the side with the rubble. Mr. Andel would have been horrified. He wouldn't have liked seeing the chains, either. Why did the fort people make the workers wear chains? Were they prisoners?

The setting sun was now turning the sky a deep red traced with purple clouds, and the valley below was covered in shadow. Jin crawled back out from between the boulders and went back to his cave, glad not to be looking at the mine anymore.

He rolled up the mat he'd slept on, with Zinde's sword inside. Then he gathered everything he'd brought with him in a rush basket after changing back into his ragged Caerda clothes. He took down the loose pile of rocks that had shielded his fire from being seen outside, kicking the ashes about. With the evidence of his stay hidden, he put on his *kebba* and peered out the cave mouth again. Yes, the sun was almost completely down. He could go.

Jin ran down the mountainside as fast as he could, the black fabric of the *kebba* flying behind him. There was just enough light still in the sky for him to see the trail, but when it was gone he'd have to wait for the moon. He also had to watch out for anyone out with a lamp. Moro thought that was unlikely, but he still had to be careful.

Panting, he reached the crossroads just as the last light faded. His feet were sore from all the rocks on the trail, but it felt good to run after being cooped up in the cave for days.

Jin looked around the crossroads as best he could in the dark. It was hard to tell, but it looked like he was alone. He crouched down to wait, gathering the *kebba* more closely around him. It got cool quickly here when the sun went down. He waited for what seemed like hours, until a fat crescent moon climbed over the mountains. By its pale light he could see a dark figure moving along the road from the village and approaching the crossroads.

"Tell me, O Darkness, do you hold within you one with a face like cheese?"

Jin grinned and stood up. "Alas, he died of old age waiting for you, donkey with three legs."

Moro chuckled. "Now, why is it you can speak with ease and grace to be insulting, but as a babbling child for all else?"

"I learn from what I hear. What news?"

Moro drew closer and lowered his voice. "It is good that you hid. There have been many *maahtik* in the village; more than usual. Zinde sent this with one of the porters bringing food." He handed Jin a small, flattish object that felt like a shard of pottery.

"A broken pot?"

Moro made an exasperated noise. "Look at it."

Jin squinted in the moonlight. Scratched on the slightly curved surface was what looked like an outline of the fort, a smaller rectangle at one corner and a squiggly line down one side. So Zinde had found a way. There were other drawings, too, which he supposed would make sense when he got inside the fort.

"Where is this?"

"There is a walled garden outside the *maaht*. The gate will be shut, but the wall is not as high around the garden and it is not guarded. Come, we must go now." They started walking down the road that led to the fort.

"Does your father know anything of Zinde's plan?"

Moro snorted. "He knows Zinde. No, I told him I

was going to see you—and I did!" His grin flashed. "He wants you to return, and so do I. I swear the last water tunnel even you would have found cramped, and I had to clear it all by myself. In the dark," he mumbled. "I am tired. If this were not to find Aba Karestal..."

"Zinde thinks the door might be there, too," Jin said without thinking.

"Door? What door?"

"A door...back to Galetan. My world, where the *maahtik* come from." The words stumbled from his mouth. Maybe he shouldn't have said anything, but if he disappeared, what would Moro think?

And what did *he* think? It wasn't like it had been at first, where everything was strange and frightening and the only person he could understand was Zinde. He liked Hasnen a'Kanahti, who worked hard and expected him to work hard, too, but was fair and never beat him. Moro and Zinde were now his friends, better than any of the friends he had in Thama. He'd even gotten used to the heat and the dust, mostly.

"The *maahtik* had to come here somehow," Moro said eventually. "But you came with the little star, in a different place." Jin had shown Moro the crystal sphere and told him what happened in the burned-out warehouse. "Did you try to go back then, the same way?"

"Yes, but it didn't work. I don't know why it worked the first time. I've never heard of magic crystals that make holes in the air, either. Have you?"

"No." Moro sounded sad. "I don't want you to leave. Why do you want to return to a place that is so cold you could die?"

"It isn't always cold," Jin protested. "And everyone says it is dangerous for the village for me to be here."

"True, but...we have hidden you so far without being found."

He was sounding truly unhappy, and Jin tried to cheer him up. "Zinde was only guessing about the door. Maybe there is nothing, and you are stuck with me forever."

If he did find a door, what did he want to do? Jin wasn't used to having choices, other than do-this-or-die. Gutter rats didn't get choices; it was what made them gutter rats.

"This is true." Moro didn't sound so sad anymore. "You have what she gave you?"

The sword. Jin nodded, and then realized Moro couldn't see him. "Wrapped in the mat."

"Good. The *maahtik* forbid us weapons and search all who enter. For her to be found with it would mean her death. Remember this—if you are about to be discovered, you must take the sword from her. And you do not know us."

"And I don't know your strange words, either."

Moro laughed softly. "*Aya*, that will not be entirely a lie." He walked in silence for a while. "What is Thama like, Jinli? Is it like the *maaht* everywhere?"

Jin grimaced, trying to find enough words he knew in Rabani to explain. "Some places. Many buildings like that, but close together. More people than...a hundred villages. Much water. A big *kanah* but not underground, we call *river*. And water falls from the sky, often."

"It does not! How can it? How does the water get up there?"

Jin shrugged. "I don't know how. It just does."

"Maybe it is magic. There must be magic everywhere, like the lightning sticks the guards have and the cave dragon of the mines."

"That's not magic," Jin scoffed. "The thing in the mine is a steam engine. It is just a machine. Anybody can use a gun, and steam engines are all over. Jinxers make things out of magic, like gems."

The road had been rising slightly as they walked, and when they reached the top of the rise, Jin could see the fort ahead, with lights in the corner towers and at the gates. Moro put a hand on Jin's shoulder.

"No more talking now. It carries on the night air."

A little farther and they left the road entirely. It took all Jin's concentration to follow the dark shadow that was Moro through the ragged scrub and rocks. The fort grew closer, until he could see the soldiers patrolling the walls. As Moro had said, he could hear voices from the fort, laughing and talking. This was good. If the people inside were noisy, he would not be heard.

Now the garden wall was in sight, and Jin could see the tops of trees above the stones. He jogged along the wall until he found what he was looking for —cracks and protruding stones in the wall. He fingered the first few. Sturdy enough, and he could get a grip. He tugged at the *kebba* and pulled it loose.

"No..." Moro whispered.

"It gets in the way," Jin whispered back. "Black is seen against pale stone, easy. Only village people wear *kebba*." He was wearing his Caerdon clothes, too, just in case someone saw him—or he found the way back to Thama. Jin slung the rolled-up mat containing the sword across his back, where it would not interfere with climbing.

Moro took the black cloth and folded it. "I will bury it here, by this flat stone. You might need it later."

Jin scrambled up the wall. If they understood Zinde's message, she would have a rope hanging near the place the north wall of the garden met the wall of the fort. The garden wall had decorative shapes on the top that made it hard to walk on, but with his bare feet and toes gripping the edges, Jin managed.

Then he got to the fort wall and stopped. There was no rope. He looked up. Nothing.

Jin glanced down at Moro. "Wrong place?" he whispered. Moro shook his head violently. Jin studied the wall more carefully. It was better made, of cut stone that showed no chinks or ridges. He could never climb that. How else could he get inside? He studied the big wooden door that opened into the garden. It was thick and studded with iron—and it was opening.

"Run! Someone is coming!"

"But you—"

"I'll hide in the tree!" Jin didn't dare drop back down from the wall on either side, but one tree had a sturdy branch he could reach from the wall. He swung himself up, hoping the darkness would cover what the leaves did not. Maybe taking off the *kebba* had been a bad idea.

A group of men came through the doorway, light streaming about them from inside the fort. They were dressed in Caerdon clothing. Jin lay flat along the branch and wrapped his arms and legs around the rough bark, doing his best to look like just another part of the tree. He could smell the scent of the flowers in the garden, sweet and heavy.

"Ah, much cooler out here. Here, girl, bring us food and some ale!"

The group spread out to some stone benches in the middle of the garden. From the way they were walking, they weren't precisely drunk, but they certainly weren't completely sober, either.

"The nights are pleasant, I grant you, but the days make this place a damned hellhole. Why we have to stay here constantly for six months at a time eludes me. Don't we have enough portallers to allow a few visits to Thama now and then?" The man who spoke was rather fat and appeared to be feeling the heat more than the rest.

A man with dark hair and a long, narrow nose gave him a frown. "The portallers are much better employed as they are...and no, we do not have enough as it is. They are very hard to find."

The fat man opened his mouth to speak, but a girl came in burdened with a heavy tray and a jug. Zinde! She was wearing a thin scarf like a *kebba* over her head and clothing, but he recognized her anyway. So that was why the rope wasn't there!

Zinde placed the tray and jug on one of the stone benches and left quickly. One of the drunk men tried to call her back, but she had already gone, maybe pretending not to hear.

"Leave the sandy chit be," said the man with the nose. "We need to discuss the mine schedule and other things the natives shouldn't hear. We are badly behind schedule with all those deaths."

One of the others groaned and refilled his mug, spilling some in the process. "Can't we just enjoy one miserable party without talking of work? You worry too much, Goront."

"It's my responsibility, and Ellins can't get his face out of his plate long enough to get the schedule back on track. The excavator has been fixed and is working quite well now, but we still need hands to sort and extract the corundum from the ore."

"Arrangements have been made," the fat man said, waving a hand holding a half-eaten fruit. "Three hundred workers were purchased in the market of Bos-Vedai. The portallers will begin transferring them to the mine tomorrow. And I fail to see how it is my fault you keep killing the sandy beggars, Goront. The expense is adding up."

"We should take over Bos-Vedai and not pay anything," Goront grumbled.

"Soldiers cost money, too, and they can't be natives—finding men who won't talk back home isn't easy, either."

"So take some of the locals, then."

"And what if they get loose and talk to their friends, eh? No, wiser heads than you have already considered this. We've got a posh thing here, if you just do your job and stop whinging about it not being easier." Ellins smiled and took a swig, making Goront's angry expression even angrier. "We can't risk anyone back home finding out about this. Everything you complain about is part of the plan to *keep* it secret. So if you can't keep your mouth shut, fill it with beer. I'm tired of listening to you."

Behind him, Jin heard a slithering sound. He'd been trying to ignore the insects crawling over him, but that noise made him look around. It wasn't a creature, though. A rope now hung over the wall of the fort.

CHAPTER 9
THE PRISONER

"Moro was right—you do climb fast," Zinde whispered, pulling up the rope when Jin had reached the top. "I apologize for the delay. I could not leave without being seen until now. Where is the sword?" She quickly coiled up the rope and hid it behind a wooden bench.

Jin tilted his head. "On my back. I saw you down in the garden. I was in the tree."

He glanced around quickly. They were at the top of the fort, a broad platform beyond the outer edge in the shape of a hollow square. A shorter wall ran along the inside of the square, and he could see the inner square went all the way to the ground. Open stairs led down to a second level, and higher walls had openings that seemed to be interior stairs as well. The interior stair entrances had torches, but the rest of the wall was dark. He didn't see anybody else there.

"Where are the guards?"

"I brought them food and drink and left it in their quarters so they would leave. They will return soon. Hurry!" Zinde tugged his arm, leading him down one of the narrow, twisting interior stairwells. "I must go back to the kitchen before I am missed. You have the map? This is the outer wall, and this is the courtyard. The kitchen is this building here. When everyone is asleep, come and unbar the little side door, the one along the inner passageway." She peered around the corner at the bottom of the stairs. "The storage areas are below. Do you see that archway? Hide there until the *maahtik* sleep."

She darted away before he could protest. Jin waited until she was gone before running himself, making sure no one was in sight. The opening of the archway was darker than the hall, which had several lamps along the walls. He debated removing one of the lamps but decided light where it was not expected would attract notice.

The steps leading down were broad and led to a short passage with a rough flagstone floor. He went slowly, allowing his eyes to adapt to the darkness, and found he could see fairly well with the light reflected down the stairs. Enough that he wanted an even better place to hide, just in case someone looked his direction.

Doors opened off the passage to the right and left. The one on the left was locked or stuck. The one on the right opened with effort, creaking, and Jin winced. Well, either someone had heard it or they hadn't. He wedged his way in the door, leaving it open just a crack. It was risky if anyone came down the stairs, but making a sound when he left was dangerous, too.

It was completely dark inside the storeroom. By feel, Jin discovered barrels; burlap sacks that appeared to have potatoes in them from the damp, earthy smell; and smooth glass bottles in a rack. He could smell onions somewhere, too.

How long did he have to wait? Zinde hadn't said. He'd heard sounds of talk and laughter as they went down the stairs, so the fort people were still celebrating. Maybe he should find a more comfortable spot to wait than crouching on the stone floor.

Jin shifted some sacks of potatoes and other lumpy things to dig out a small depression in the pile of supplies. It wasn't very comfortable, so even though he would doze off, the lumps would make him wake up again.

He had just lifted another sack out of the way in an effort to improve things when he heard the door behind him creak and a muttered curse as a beam of light entered the dark room. Jin dived for the hiding place and flattened himself, hoping his ragged clothes would blend in with the burlap sacks.

From behind the sacks Jin could not see the door, but he could see the beam of light coming closer and hear the stumbling footsteps. He held his breath, sure he would be discovered. But the light kept going, stopping at the far wall. Now he could see the person's face—it was Goront, the long-nosed man from the garden! He was constantly looking over his shoulder, beads of sweat forming on his forehead even though the storeroom was cool. He took a small bag from inside his jacket and removed one of the wine bottles, tucking the bag somewhere behind the rack and then replacing the bottle carefully.

Goront then hurried out, closing the door softly behind him. Jin waited for a while, and when the man did not return, he got up. He couldn't see the rack of wine bottles, but by taking them out one by one and feeling around, he eventually found the little bag. It was heavy, and the contents clinked slightly. Why had Goront hidden it, and what was inside?

Jin went to the door for light. He opened it carefully, and this time it did not make any sound. In fact, he couldn't hear any sound outside, either. The singing had stopped. Was it safe to find Zinde now?

He went cautiously up the stairs. Still no sound of voices. His heart pounding, Jin crept down the hallway where Zinde had gone. For a panicked moment he thought he saw a moving shadow, but it was only a guttering lamp that soon went out.

There was the small door shown on the map, and it was barred. Jin put both hands underneath the bar and slowly eased it up. The kitchen was faintly lit by the embers of the cooking fire. Sleeping bodies were scattered everywhere, and he wondered how he would find Zinde in their midst. But then one head lifted, looking at the door, and Zinde stood and silently made her way out.

"We should put the bar back down," she whispered. "Sometimes the guards check."

With both of them it was easier to lower the bar without making any noise. Zinde stared at his hands on the bar. "What's that you have?"

Jin looked at the bag he was holding. He'd almost forgotten about it. "I don't know. There was this man in the garden, I think he is in charge of the mine. He came to the storeroom I was in and hid this, and I wanted to see what was in it." Jin loosened the neck of the little bag and shook out the contents—and nearly dropped them in shock. Fiery gems filled his palm, glowing with light, red and gold and green.

Zinde gasped. "He's stealing from his own people?"

Jin hastily stuffed the gems back in the bag and tied the neck, stuffing it in his pocket. Was it stealing if you took something from someone who stole it first? "So that's what's in the mine. What should I do with it?"

"My father will know." Zinde's face was determined behind the gauze veil. "Give me the sword and we will find him."

Jin backed away, keeping one hand on the rope that held the rolled-up mat on his back. "If anyone sees you holding it here, you'll get in trouble. Besides, you don't need it now."

Zinde made an irritated sound and stamped her foot. "I want it *before* I need it. There might not be time to get it out."

"Don't make noise! We should be looking for your father instead of wasting time."

That made Zinde spin around and run off, Jin following. They darted around two sides of the fort, occasionally hiding in the shadows as the sentries on the top of the wall came in view.

"Do you even know how to use a sword?" Zinde whispered fiercely as they hid behind a pillar.

Jin scowled. "Do you?"

"My father showed me once." She pointed to an arched doorway that led away from the open walk of the fort and up more stairs. "Don't laugh at me!"

Zinde could just barely lift the sword, so he couldn't really understand how she could use it. He also had a suspicion it took a little more practice than one try to use a sword. Jin stifled his amusement. "Moro was right about you."

Zinde elbowed him in the side. He was about to object, and then he heard snoring. Peering around the corner of the stairwell, he saw a guard slumped in a chair. A mug and a plate beside him showed he had also been taking part in the festivities, perhaps too much. His rifle was propped against the wall next to him.

"The cells are that way," Zinde whispered in Jin's ear, pointing.

Their bare feet made no sound as they crept past the guard. He was stationed at the entrance to a hallway with three doors, each with a small barred window up high. Even Zinde wasn't tall enough to look through the windows, so she helped Jin grab the bars and pull himself up to look inside.

The first cell was empty. The second was occupied, with someone sleeping in the narrow cot. Strangely, the cell also had some furniture—a dresser and a chair. Jin wasn't sure about how these things were done, but he had always thought a prison cell wouldn't have chairs.

"There's someone inside, but I can't see their face," he said softly to Zinde.

She stuck out her chin and stood on her tiptoes. "Aba!" she said in a fierce whisper. "Aba!"

There was no response. Jin nudged her over to the third cell. It was empty, too.

Zinde's shoulders sagged. Jin wondered what he could say. Maybe there were other cells in the fort they could search.

And then they heard a man's voice, whispering as quietly as they had, saying, "Who is there?" But he wasn't speaking Rabani. It was Caerda, and he sounded like one of the genteel.

Jin froze for a moment, fear making his blood run cold, then he grabbed Zinde's wrist and pulled hard. She couldn't be seen here. He'd promised Moro to look after her. It was a *maahtik* in that cell! It was too late for him; the man could see him from the little barred window. But Zinde, still in her dark veil, was next to the cell door. If the man did not look straight down, she might escape notice.

"Come back! I mean you no harm."

Jin hesitated, frantically gesturing to get Zinde to creep under the door window and escape. Instead, she moved behind him, trying to untie the rolled-up mat on his back, and he couldn't stop her without letting the man know she was there. Maybe he should distract him.

"Who are you?"

"Good heavens, it's a boy...and you're from Galetan. Why did they bring you here, of all places?"

Jin came closer to the window, puzzled. "Nobody brought me. Why are you locked up? Sir." Who would dare lock up a genteel? Even the billies didn't do that.

"Don't argue—you have to go before those blackguards discover you are here. They'll kill you, lad."

"Do not threaten my friend, or I will kill you myself!" Zinde had the sword in her hands now and was pointing it at the barred window. Jin, wincing, saw the man's eyes widen in surprise.

"Young lady, I was merely trying to warn him. Take care and lower your voice, or we'll have the guard on us. Why are the two of you wandering about here?"

"We aren't wandering about, we are looking for my father," Zinde said irritably.

"I haven't seen anyone locked up here but myself, save a few drunk guards now and then." The man hesitated. "May I ask your father's name?"

Zinde gave Jin a worried glance, and Jin shrugged. The man was being polite and hadn't yelled for the guard. It was all very odd.

"Inden Karestal," Zinde said reluctantly.

The man groaned, his face twisting like something hurt, and his head dipped. Then he looked up again.

"Miss Karestal. I wish I had good news to give you."

Zinde made a small noise in the back of her throat that sounded like pain felt. Jin put a hand on her shoulder, not knowing what else he could do. It must be hard to have done so much and have nothing to show for it at the end.

"Please do not be distressed. When I last saw him he was alive—but he was helping me in my...investigations, so when I was captured, they took him, too. They must have imprisoned him somewhere else. Since I am in his debt, whatever help I can offer you is yours. Unfortunately, I will need some assistance in escaping for that offer to be of any value." He gave a wry smile, and then his gaze went to Jin. "Now tell me, lad, how did you get to this world from Caerdon if nobody brought you? Because only jinxers can travel between worlds."

CHAPTER 10
SIR MARIST

Jin stared at the man, stunned. He heard the words but they made no sense.

"I'm no jinxer!" Maybe the man was crazy. They'd have to lock up a crazy genteel, wouldn't they?

They had all been keeping their voices low, so when a normal voice spoke from outside in the courtyard, it was clear. The man turned his head sharply, looking at the barred window on the wall of his cell.

"No time—they are changing the guard. Go, now! Hide and come back when you can!"

Jin and Zinde ran. The sleeping guard was beginning to stir.

"I'll shut you in the kitchen again," Jin panted.

Zinde shook her head. "You'll be seen. Don't worry—I'll stay out of sight until they open the door. Nobody in the kitchen will be looking for me right away, and the guards will see the bar is still down. Where will you go?"

"I have an idea." Jin held out his hand for the sword, and Zinde reluctantly let go. Jin raced off up the stairs to the top of the fort, struggling to put the sword back in the rolled-up mat. It was still dark outside, which helped. First he needed to find the rope Zinde had used to let him in. There were guards on the wall and more walking about because of the change, but they still needed light to see—and he could see them.

He found the pile of rope still hidden under the bench and wound it around himself and over one shoulder. He could see now that Zinde had knotted it together from shorter pieces. Now, where were the cells? Jin hunkered down beside the low parapet of the wall and tried to retrace the way he had come. The cell had one window, with three bars in it, and the window faced the inside courtyard of the fort. There were three cells next to each other with the same arrangement.

The fort didn't have any of his favorite climbing helpers like drainpipes—but then Moro had not believed him when he mentioned rain. Maybe it didn't rain here.

There. Only one part of the fort had three barred windows in a row. Jin groaned. The cells were right beneath one of the long walkways the guards patrolled. How could he possibly avoid being seen?

He could just see a pale light on the horizon. If he stayed where he was, he would be seen anyway. He watched, his stomach knotting with worry. The soldiers walked, but they had a set time. Only the ones at the corners had torches. In between, there was only the light from the sky. If he moved fast, while the walking guard was at one end and looking the other way, he could get to the middle section, where he needed to be, without being seen.

No time to think about it. He got the rope out as he ran, making a loop in one end and folding the whole length in half. The sky was getting lighter. Jin hid behind a barrel and watched the soldier go by. The parapet was made of stone blocks with gaps between them, like a row of old teeth. When the soldier was far enough but still facing away, Jin darted to the parapet and dropped the middle of the rope around one of the stone blocks and swung over the side, holding both sections of the rope.

He hadn't guessed exactly and had to swing a bit as he dropped, but he was, with a bit of effort, able to grab the bars of the middle cell window. He fed the end with the loop inside the window and hissed.

Strong hands grabbed the rope and pulled. Jin stood on the sill of the window and held the iron bar, taking his weight off the rope to give slack.

"It's secured," the man whispered. "What on earth are you doing, young man? I can't get out that way."

Jin took hold of the rope, just in case, and wiggled his shoulder and head through the bars. The man had to pull him through all the way, and then Jin hastily drew in the rest of the rope. Hopefully none of the soldiers had noticed it when it was wrapped around the stone block—and now it was gone.

"I figure nobody's gonna look for someone inside a cell," Jin managed, still panting. "And I'm small enough to get out again."

The man gave a wry smile. From what Jin could see in the dim light, he was tall, thin, with dark hair and a beard, and an expression on his face like he found his troubles amusing. His shirt looked like quality but it was dirty and torn, and he wasn't wearing a coat or even a vest. "You are an enterprising lad. Fortunate for us both they did not plan on imprisoning someone your size when they built this place, no? But you need to hide. They will be bringing food soon."

The only place Jin could conceal himself was

under the bed, and he had to take off the mat roll with the sword and duck under the metal braces that held the legs. The man rearranged his blanket so it fell over the edge, and lay down as if he were still sleeping. Jin couldn't help flinching when the door scraped open with a jangle of keys. The man pretended sleep even while the tin plate with food was dropped on the floor, and Jin held motionless until the footsteps faded down the hall.

"We can speak now, if we're quiet. I think some introductions are in order, don't you?"

Jin wiggled a little closer to the head of the bed. "I'm Jin, sir."

"A pity we meet in such circumstances, but nevertheless a pleasure to make your acquaintance, and Miss Karestal, also. I am Sir Janal Marist, of the Metropol."

Jin froze. Not just a genteel, but a nob! "W-what's a metropol?"

Sir Marist chuckled softly. "I daresay they don't often come your way. Just as the more general officers of the law—I believe they are commonly called 'billies' or 'brassers'—take care of crimes among ordinary people, there are those who perform the same function at a higher level. I was assigned the task of investigating the curious activities of a certain jinxer company, Gariard. It has managed to swallow up several smaller companies of a similar nature, and not always in a legal manner. Jinxers have remarkable abilities, but even for jinxers, Gariard showed an astonishing ability to profit, and, er, more than one curiously missing employee. And then we learned that the profit itself might not be entirely legitimate."

"But...sir. They've locked you up!" Jin couldn't

think of anyone who would dare lock up a billy, and a billy that was a nob in addition—how crazy were these people?

"And very inconvenient it is, too. I suppose it is fortunate they haven't killed me, but they don't need to. I can't return to Thama and report them—but they don't know how much I discovered or if I managed to get word out before they caught me, despite all their questioning. And if I *had* gotten word out, and it is suspected they killed me, they would be in a great deal of trouble for that alone." Sir Marist swung his legs down from the bed and picked up the plate of food. "As to what they are so worried I found out...I haven't the slightest notion. Why they need to come here to transmute their goods escapes me, unless they need large amounts of sand. Hungry, Jin?"

"I could eat, I guess." Jin was always hungry, but he felt reluctant to take Sir Marist's food. There wasn't very much of it.

"Help yourself—I've quite lost my appetite. Now, why don't you tell me how you managed to get here?"

Jin took a piece of hard cheese from the plate and told Sir Marist his story. He left nothing out, even the crystal sphere, but he didn't mention he still had it with him. Sir Marist seemed friendly, but he was still a genteel.

"And that is how you met the redoubtable Miss Karestal, I presume. From what you have described to me, you are most certainly a jinxer—at least the kind they call a portaller. Jinxers are a secretive lot, so we don't know much about them. One thing I've learned is they can travel magically using those spheres. What I did not know, and which got me in this predicament, is they can travel between worlds. When I went nosing around Gariard and their transports, it never even occurred to me. I thought no matter where I ended up, I could return to Thama, you see."

Jin chewed thoughtfully on the cheese. It had a sharp flavor and a tough rind. Strange as it was, he supposed Sir Marist was right. He had opened a portal. Which made him a jinxer. *But I don't feel any different...*

"So why couldn't I do this...portal thing back to Thama, then?"

"An excellent question. I have been pondering how I got here myself, and something you said reminded me. I suspect you may need the sphere to do the trick, and maybe a specific one depending on where you wish to go. The previous portals I had gone through, ones that stayed in Caerdon, had been opened by a jinxer holding a sphere that looked smoky grey, with threads of bright green. The one that opened a portal to this world looked like fire."

"Oh!" Jin sat up in excitement, hitting his head painfully on the bottom of the bed. "Like the one I found, you mean?"

"Precisely. Perhaps the type of sphere limits what they can do. I still have not discovered how they create their gems, which is what I was originally investigating."

Jin remembered the little bag he had found and pulled it out. "Maybe it isn't magic for that. They got mines in the mountains. I hid in a cave there for a few days. They've got a steam engine, and these people all in chains doing digging. And I also heard one of the *maahtik*—I mean, the fort people—say he needed more workers because so many had died and they were buying them from Bos-Vedai. Three hundred, he said. I don't think they could all be jinxers, do you? He hid this, too. Maybe that is what they are mining," he said, holding out the bag from under the bed for Sir Marist to take.

Sir Marist took it and was silent for so long Jin wondered if he had said something wrong. He peeked from under the bed. Sir Marist had a hard, angry expression on his face, and his fists were clenched on his knees.

Jin ducked back into the shadows, wishing he could run. "Was it wrong to take them? I didn't mean to do wrong. I'll put them back."

Sir Marist stirred, and his hands relaxed. "I'm not angry at you, Jin. Far from it. I knew from what Karestal told me that his people were being mistreated by Gariard, but I did not know the extent of it. Now it is even more important that we escape and bring this information back to the Metropol."

"How can we do that, sir?" Jin felt a wave of relief. Sir Marist not only wasn't mad at him, but was planning to take Jin back to Thama. It seemed strange to plan anything with a nob, but Sir Marist was a strange nob. He didn't seem to care Jin was a gutter rat at all, and he was sad about Zinde's father—like he was a friend. Maybe he would help Zinde find her father.

"I'll need to get out of this cell, for one thing. The guard doesn't have the key—there's a man that comes with him to open the cell when they bring my food, and he has it. Then we need to find where they keep their portal spheres and hope you can do what you did before."

"I think Zinde knows where they keep them."

"Excellent! The two of you make an effective team, I must say. Now, we won't be able to do much until dark. I suggest you get some sleep while you can."

CHAPTER 11
ESCAPE

Jin tried to sleep, but the cell was hot and stuffy and the underside of the bed cramped and full of hard, poky bits he kept rolling into, and the sword took up too much of the space for comfort. Sounds from outside kept waking him up in fear he had been discovered. He also found himself thinking of Zinde and Moro, and Une Karestal, and the other people of the village.

Part of him wanted to go back to Thama, where things were not so strange. But he didn't want to leave the people he'd met here, either. It didn't matter. He didn't belong here—and he'd promised to help Zinde find her father. Mr. Karestal wasn't here in the fort, so he'd probably been taken to Thama if he was still alive. Jin had to go back to Thama anyway, just for that. And Sir Marist needed to go back, too.

That point settled, he dozed off for a while. The arrival of dinner woke him again, and he watched what he could from under the bed. A guard brought in the tin plate and handed it to Sir Marist, but Jin could hear two others outside—he recognized Goront's voice, and there was another who spoke in a deep rumble he couldn't understand.

"No, we aren't bringing the chair back. The guard before you was found asleep. We can't have you slacking off. No one is allowed to speak to the prisoner, do you understand? And someone thought they saw one of the savages wandering around last night as well." Another deep mumble, sounding unhappy. "It can't be helped. We don't have enough guards as it is, and a shipment goes out tomorrow. I'll be busy with that. Someone will relieve you before dawn, that's all I can promise. Do your job and stop complaining, or I'll have you sacked!"

Dinner was a more substantial meal, a cup of thick soup and some of the local flat bread, along with some festival cakes that had gotten burned on the bottom. Jin didn't mind. He'd eaten worse, and even burned, the cakes were quite good.

"Right. What do you plan to do, once you wiggle out the window tonight?"

Jin shrugged, even though Sir Marist couldn't see him. "Get Zinde out of the kitchen. I figure she might know where Goront keeps the keys. It was that man who came that has them, right?"

"Correct. He's in charge—either of the whole fort, or part of it. I haven't figured it out, and for some strange reason they are reluctant to answer my questions." Amusement tinged Sir Marist's voice. "On rare occasions he will hand over the keys to someone else, but usually he is the only one to unlock my door—and he greatly resents the trouble, I can assure you. Which leads me to think he has been ordered to do so. From what he was saying to the unfortunate guard, it sounds as if he will be quite busy. I only hope it will not involve taking the same set of keys we need."

"Yeah, that would be bad. He better have the keys to where the other spheres are, too. How else will we get them?"

Sir Marist coughed. "I, ah, may be able to obtain them without the key."

"What, you're a twiddler? But...but you're a nob!" Jin was bewildered. He knew plenty of twiddlers, but he didn't believe the genteel even knew the word. Or would have any need to open locks without keys.

"I never said I was a very good one—but yes, I've had the training. With the right tools, I can handle most locks. One of the best, er, came over to our side, shall we say, and gave us lessons. I'm afraid that in my line of work, we occasionally need to make use of criminal methods to fight crime."

"Ooer!" Jin was unable to say anything else for a moment, stunned by this revelation. "So this crack twiddler that taught you, he works for Metropol, too?"

"You sound shocked. I assure you, he tolerates us quite well, and we all hold him in great esteem."

"Ooer," Jin said again. This Metropol bunch must be an odd lot. Crazy as ducks, from the sounds of it.

Sir Marist got up off the bed and his footsteps went to the window, then came back. "It's starting to get dark. We should get you out of here as soon as possible, so you have plenty of time to find those keys."

He started to pull out the rope from under the bed. Jin crawled out, remembering to take the rolled-up mat with Zinde's sword with him. He held it in one hand, looking at it and then at Sir Marist, thinking.

"Maybe you should have this. If there's trouble."

Sir Marist glanced at him. "What's that?"

"It's Zinde's sword. Her father's, really. The

people get punished if they are found with weapons, they told me. And...and if it's here with you, she can't get at it. She'd believe you could take it from me, anyway."

Sir Marist stifled a chuckle. "I see. You could also encourage her to think I took it to ensure you came back to release me. She is, after all, a most determined young lady and might forget me in the excitement of seeking her father."

Jin smiled with relief, seeing he understood. "She does get...a bit stubborn, sometimes, I guess—but she and her mother have been real good to me. I promised Mo...I promised a friend I'd look after her."

"But of course. I give you my word I will take the greatest care of Miss Karestal's sword." Sir Marist bowed. "Ready, lad?"

It was harder getting out than going in. Jin had scrapes on his face that bled sluggishly by the time he escaped. He dropped quickly to the ground of the courtyard and stepped back, waving to Sir Marist. He couldn't see him, but the rope disappeared back into the cell window, and Jin ran off.

The fort seemed quiet, and at first he thought it was only in comparison to the festival the previous night. Then, after reaching the kitchen side door, he realized the only guards he had seen were on the walls. Something Goront had said now made sense. No one could come and replace the guard at Sir Marist's cell because they were all busy elsewhere.

Jin lifted the bar of the kitchen door with great care and opened it slowly. Zinde was lying across the doorway inside, and silently rose and slipped through the narrow opening.

"I was worried you would not come," she

whispered. "They wanted me to leave tonight, but I pretended to be afraid of walking back to the village in the dark, and they allowed me to stay until morning."

"We need to find the keys to Sir Marist's cell," Jin whispered back. "You remember, the man we found? I talked to him. He thinks he can find your father, but we have to get him out first." Jin described Goront as best he could.

Zinde frowned, her brow wrinkling in thought. She was wearing her more usual scarf instead of the long, full one of the previous night.

"There is only one *maahtik* like what you say. He tells the one in charge of the kitchen what to do, and holds his head so." Zinde tilted her head back, looking down her nose. "We are as dust to his feet, in his eyes. If he has the keys, we must look in the clerk's rooms. He has an office there."

She led the way to the interior courtyard, staying in the deep shadows. Jin had thought the clerk's rooms would be in the fort itself, but instead there was a smaller, separate building in the courtyard. Zinde tried the door, but it was locked. The lower floor had large windows, but they had metal grilles covering them.

Jin stepped back and looked up. It was a small building of a kind that could be found anywhere in Thama, so it was rather strange here. While it had a sloped roof, the top floor was not as long as the lower section, leaving a small balcony ledge with a low wall about it. Motion caught his eye, and he froze—but after watching, he decided it was just curtains moving in the night breeze.

He stared, thinking. If the curtains were moving inside the room, one of the windows had to be open.

"I need to get up there," he whispered to Zinde.

They circled the building again. The walls were well-made stone, with few handholds. There was a narrow shelf of trim between the two floors, but it was too high for him to jump and reach it, and even if he had the rope still in Sir Marist's cell, there was nothing to catch it on.

Then Jin looked at the window grilles again. He could climb *those*, if he could reach them. And with Zinde giving him a boost, he could. The metal grille had hard edges that bit into his hands, but he ignored the pain. Just a little farther and he could grab the trim.

He'd picked a window close to the balcony. Jin gripped the stone trim with one hand and pulled, testing his hold. His hand was sweaty with effort, and it slipped. He wiped his hand hastily on his shirt and tried again, in a different place. Good enough.

Taking a deep breath, he pulled up with all his strength and swung his feet up and to the side. His toes hit stone and he stifled a grunt of pain. One more time.

One foot found the edge of the low wall. He wiggled it farther over, letting one leg take more weight, then got his other foot in position. Jin didn't dare look down. If he fell here, he'd land on the stone courtyard.

More squirming and his knees were over. Then he could shift and get both hands on the trim and push. He fell over the wall, curling up to muffle the sound as best he could. If someone was still inside...

The upstairs floor was dark and appeared empty. Two long windows, like doors, faced the balcony. The curtain Jin had seen moving was pulled across the window-doors, and one edge had gotten caught between them, preventing the latch from catching. Using his fingernails, Jin was able to pull the door open.

The room was full of furniture, boxes, and cabinets. It would take him all night to search this, especially if he didn't have a light. He needed Zinde's help.

Jin felt his way to the stair, which went down one wall. He made sure to walk on the wall side to prevent any creaking. Then he had to figure out the door latch and hiss to catch Zinde's attention.

"Where should we look?" he asked.

"The upper room. Many people come here during the day; he would not keep keys where they could be found." Zinde started to run up the stairs, then stopped. "Where is my sword?"

"I left it with Sir Marist. I...I couldn't fit through the window with it, and I saw a guard..."

Zinde stared at him. "What window? You lost it, didn't you!"

"No! I hid in Sir Marist's cell all day. The bars in the window had enough space for me to get through." His stomach sank. If he could get in with the sword, he could get out with it, too, and Zinde would know that. "There isn't time. The keys must be upstairs, and there's too much for me to look through. Come on!" Jin waited for Zinde to figure it out and get mad about the sword, but instead she rolled her eyes and kept going up the stairs.

"See the clever Jinli!" she said in Rabani.

By now Jin's eyes had adapted to the dark of the room, and he could see what he was searching. From what Sir Marist had said, the keys to the cell would not be on a larger ring with other keys that were used frequently. A smaller bunch of keys—perhaps just three, to match the three cells. Jin was also looking for some thin wire that Sir Marist would use for the twiddling, somehow.

He found a paper of pins and a metal instrument made of two legs joined together at one end. Each end of the leg had a long, sharp metal point. He had no idea what it was used for, but it might work.

"*Ala!* I have hunted!" Zinde held up a knotted leather string with three keys tied along its length. "Behind the draperies."

"I sure wouldn't have thought to look there," Jin said. "They look like the right ones, too." The lock to the cell had an opening that was rectangular, instead of with a round part at the top like all the locks he'd ever seen. "We need something to deal with the guard, or he will yell when we open the door."

Zinde gave him a look. "If I had my sword..."

"No, he could still shout for help. He's probably asleep now, but how can we get Sir Marist out of the cell without waking him?"

"Why should he sleep?"

Jin explained how the guard had been left without a replacement for a long time. "He didn't sound very happy about it, and he knew Goront was going to be away for hours."

Zinde looked at the drapes thoughtfully. "If he sleeps, we can make him sleep more."

Her plan was simple. Someone would notice the missing drapes, but Jin knew Sir Marist disappearing from his cell would also raise the alarm. Zinde took one of the heavier curtains and folded it in her arms, and Jin found a heavy metal candlestick. They hurried down the stairs. With all the running about, the night was half gone.

There were still only a handful of guards around the fort, and those on the walls. Jin edged up the stairs to the hall with the cells and peered around the corner. Just as he'd expected, the guard was slumped against the wall, asleep. He waved Zinde forward.

She held the curtain in front of her, glancing behind to see where Jin was with the candlestick in both hands. With a quick flick of her wrists, the fabric wrapped over the head of the sleeping guard and over his arms. Zinde wrapped her own arms around him tightly, immobilizing him. The guard thrashed and struggled, suddenly awake, but before he could utter a sound, Jin hit him hard on the head with the candlestick, and he slumped back down, unconscious.

Jin took the string of keys from his pocket, fear making him clumsy. The second key on the string opened the lock to the cell. Sir Marist was already standing in the door, Zinde's sword in his hand. He was smiling.

"I knew I could rely on you. What did you...ah, I see. Were you able to find the wire?" Jin held out the paper of pins and the metal device. "Pins and a compass! Excellent. That should do admirably. Now, let's see about getting back to Thama."

CHAPTER 12
OPENING THE WAY

Sir Marist glanced down the hallway at the unconscious guard. "Quickly—let's get him out of sight."

The guard was a heavy man, and it took all three of them to get him inside the cell. Sir Marist removed the guard's jacket and belt before ripping his blanket into strips and tying the man up, adding a gag as well. "That should hold him." He put on the jacket and started to arrange the belt.

"Why do you do this?" Zinde asked. Jin saw, with a sinking feeling, she had recovered her sword.

"With luck we can avoid being seen, but if our luck runs out, the longer I look like a guard instead of an escaped prisoner, the better off we will be," said Sir Marist. He went out of the cell, locked it, and picked up the guard's fallen rifle. "And of course, I am escorting two dangerous criminals. Speaking of which, dangerous criminals should not have their weapons visible." He grinned as Zinde, grumbling, managed to hide her sword under her robe. "Now, Miss Karestal, can you guide us to where you saw those spheres?"

Zinde turned and led them down to the ground level of the fort, then around the central courtyard to an area Jin had not been to. As they went, Jin would run ahead and peer around corners to see if anyone was there, and then wave the others on. Unlike before, he saw two guards, but they were bored and not paying attention. It was not hard to get past them.

The fact that there were still guards here must mean something needed watching, even more than Sir Marist. Jin felt his stomach tighten with excitement.

Zinde headed for an archway with stairs going down, similar to the one with the storerooms. This one, however, gave access to a longer, better-lit hallway with several iron-bound doors on either side. Jin watched the upper hall from the top of the stairs and made sure no one had seen them while Zinde and Sir Marist descended.

"I was standing where Jin is now," Zinde said softly, and pointed to the farthest iron door. "This door was open. A *maahtik* held a tray covered with cloth, and many spheres were on it. Another *maahtik* was there and reaching for one of the spheres."

Sir Marist nodded. "Right. You two stay out of sight by the bottom of the stairs, and let me know if someone comes down. This looks like a tricky one." He frowned at the iron door, taking out the pins and the compass.

Jin alternated between watching the top of the stairs for any movement and glancing at Sir Marist, who had bent some of the pins and was carefully inserting them into the lock. Working with careful concentration, his face contorting with effort, he lifted one pin at a time while simultaneously placing the long point of the compass in the lock.

Voices sounded up the stairs. Jin hissed softly to alert Sir Marist, and then he and Zinde flattened themselves against the wall next to the entrance to the stairs. Sir Marist turned away from the door and stood at attention, just like a guard would. Jin watched, heart pounding, as booted feet came in view —and walked by. He wondered what time it was. Goront had made it sound like everyone would be busy elsewhere until dawn, but it could be close to dawn now. He tried to remember how the sky had looked when they had passed the courtyard.

"That's it! Come, let's take a look." Sir Marist was gesturing sharply. The iron door was open. Zinde and Jin darted over and followed him inside. "We must be careful—there is no way to open this door from the inside, but I don't want to leave it visibly ajar, either." He glanced outside again, reaching up and to one side. "There. Less light for them, more for us. Solves two problems at once, eh?" He was holding a lantern. "See if you can find something to prop the door open."

The room was very different from any of the others in the fort Jin had seen. It was not very large, and the floor was wood instead of stone. Cabinet doors lined the walls, but the cabinets were built in instead of separate items of furniture and made of unpainted metal. All were locked.

"There's gotta be hundreds of 'em," Jin whispered, a sinking feeling in his stomach. "Which one has the spheres?"

Zinde looked around the room. "I could not see which was open." She took out her sword and placed the blade in the gap between the door and the frame. There was nothing else in the room to use.

"Perhaps there is some kind of mark or label," Sir Marist said, but he didn't sound like he believed it. Jin started looking anyway.

If Zinde had seen something that looked like a

tray, maybe it was one of the shallow drawers. One section of the wall had several of the shallow drawers, one on top of the other. Jin ran his fingers over them, looking for scratches on the lock or some other sign that the drawer was used.

Instead, he felt warmth. It felt familiar, and he reached for the crystal sphere hidden in his coat. As soon as his fingers touched it, the feeling of warmth increased.

"Here. I think...I think they are in these."

Sir Marist gave him a puzzled look but came over with the bent pins in his hand. This lock was even more difficult than the one for the door, Jin could tell, but the drawer eventually opened. Inside were ten golden spheres, just like the one Jin had, nestled in cushioned silk holes.

"I don't think that's what we need," Sir Marist said. "The gold ones should be for travel to this world. I wonder why they have them here, then?" He shook his head and applied his tools to the next drawer.

The spheres inside were a smoky green, and one of the holes in the silk cushion was empty.

"Now that is the color I recall seeing," Sir Marist observed with a satisfied tone. "Give it a try, lad. We don't have much time, I fear."

Jin reached for one of the green spheres. It felt cool and silky to the touch. But how could he make it work? He still didn't know how he'd done it the first time.

Zinde tapped Jin on the shoulder. "I want to take the others," she said very softly in Rabani. "If they are used by the *maahtik* to travel, perhaps it will hinder them in chasing us if the spheres are gone."

Jin stepped away to let her empty the drawers behind him. He held up the sphere and tried to remember what he had done in the burned-out warehouse. He'd stared at the crystal sphere, thinking of how pretty it was, and how it looked like fire, and then the hole in the air had appeared.

This time, nothing happened. The more he focused on the sphere, the more his head hurt. "Maybe this one is broken," Jin said, feeling embarrassed. Or he was, somehow. Not good enough to be a real jinxer.

Zinde was staring at him, her eyes wide. "You...I saw a shadow form. There." Zinde pointed. She regarded Jin with awe. "The edges glowed!"

So he *had* done something. But there was no opening.

Sir Marist rubbed his chin. "Let's think about this. We're below ground level here. If the portals in one place here always open to the same place in the other world, there must be some kind of correspondence. Perhaps it won't work if you're trying to reach a place that's underground. Let's try somewhere else."

He picked up the rifle, which had been left against the wall, and headed for the door, poking his head out cautiously.

Jin knew something was wrong when Sir Marist stiffened and immediately darted out, closing the door behind him. Zinde gave Jin a wide-eyed, frightened look, and they both darted to the wall with the door and flattened themselves against it. Jin didn't dare even whisper to Zinde, and he felt his heart pounding. What could they do to help Sir Marist now?

The door was still slightly ajar, with the sword

blade holding it open, and he could hear voices.

"What are you doing here?" It sounded like Goront. Jin winced. If he was back, the other guards would be back, too.

"Thowt I heard sommat, and lamp's out," Sir Marist said, sounding remarkably like a Southey dockworker. Jin blinked in astonishment. He didn't know a genteel could talk like that.

"I don't recognize you."

"Just started, sor."

"You're not supposed to be here, not without a staff escort. I'll overlook it this once, but don't do it again. Now be off with you."

Jin heard the jangle of keys, and gulped. There was nowhere to hide, no weapons...except the sword.

Zinde had already bent to retrieve it. Jin nudged her, jerking his head toward the door, and put one hand on the edge where it was ajar.

"Wait, you...come back! Was this—"

Jin yanked the door open, hard. Goront stumbled through the doorway and fell to his knees on the floor, the keys jangling on the stone. Jin snatched them away and picked them up, while Zinde had the sword at the man's throat.

"Be silent," she hissed. Goront gaped at her, his lower lip shaking and his eyes bulging in his face.

From the open door Jin saw a hand gesturing urgently. He tugged Zinde's elbow, pulling her away and out of the room before shutting the door firmly, making sure it was locked again.

"Well that's torn it," Sir Marist said, his face grim. "We have to get out of here before he's missed or someone hears him yelling." He headed for the stairs at a run.

"I can go out the main gate alone," Zinde said, "but they will not let a guard leave the *maaht* without questioning him. What will you do?"

Jin's first thought was the rope, but it was in the cell with the guard, and it was too far away to get it quickly. Now at the top of the stairs, he could see faint light in the sky from the central courtyard. Even if he could get the rope, they would be seen on the walls.

Then he remembered a different wall that did not require a rope. "Zinde, you get out and go around the fort, by the garden. We'll go over the wall there." He snagged the sword from Zinde, who for once did not protest. She darted off, and Jin ran for the small door that led to the walled garden on the other side of the fort.

Sir Marist ran behind him. They passed a group of guards who looked tired and dirty, coming from the direction Zinde had gone. They only showed mild interest as Sir Marist went by, but they stared at Jin as if he were a ghost.

"Halt!" Jin just ran faster, terror giving him speed. A loud bang came from behind, and stone splinters cracked from the wall. The guards were shooting at them! Another bang, and Sir Marist gasped.

"You get the door. I'll hold them off." His voice was tight, and when Jin glanced at him, his face was tight with pain. Sir Marist unslung the rifle he'd stolen from the guard, pulled back the bolt, and fired.

Jin shook himself and shoved at the bar to the garden door as hard as he could. The bar jumped free. "It's open!"

They burst into the garden. Sir Marist was limping badly, and Jin could see blood on one leg. "I don't think I can climb the wall..." Sir Marist protested.

"The tree...use that!"

Jin scrambled up to the branch that overhung the wall quickly, tossing the sword over the wall and reaching back to help Sir Marist. Once in the tree, his injury did not slow him as much. He managed to grasp the decorations on the top of the wall and swing himself up, and then follow Jin to a place where he could dangle on the other side and jump down.

Sir Marist groaned and stumbled as he landed, nearly falling. Jin helped him up again, found the sword, and they ran into the shadows as fast as they could. Jin heard shouting from the fort, and then a loud clanging noise. Someone was sounding the alarm!

A dark, swiftly moving shape joined them, and Jin recognized Zinde. Her scarf was coming loose and she was grinning.

"Where can we hide?" Sir Marist was panting, and the entire leg of his trousers was dark with blood now. "I don't know the area around the fort at all."

"Ho, cheese-face!"

Sir Marist gasped, raising the rifle in his hands at the sound of the voice. Jin pushed it aside.

"No, it is a friend!"

In the dawn light he could see a bush, large enough to hide them. He tugged Sir Marist over and made him crouch down. Moro was there, wrapped in his dark *kebba*.

"You found Aba Karestal?"

"No, this is someone else. He thinks he knows where Zinde's father is, though, and we helped him escape."

"I used my sword." Zinde sounded smug. "Where is it?"

Jin sighed and handed it back. "We have to move. They will be sending guards after us. Sir Marist is hurt and can't run."

"Please don't go to the village," Moro said. "It will bring trouble. They will punish us. The nearest place to hide is the mountains. Can he go that far?"

Jin translated for Sir Marist, who nodded, wincing. "I will avoid the village. I am here to help, after all. I am afraid I am too weak to reach the mountains before they catch us. Try again, Jin. I fear I see our pursuers in the distance. Someone on the wall must have seen where we went."

The sphere! Jin fumbled in his pocket. What had he done with it? All he had was his own golden sphere. It must have fallen out when he climbed the wall. "Zinde, do you still have the others?"

She reached into the folds of her robes and untwisted a fold of cloth she had used to carry the extra spheres. Jin picked out a smoky green one. It tingled and felt cool against his fingers.

It was hard to concentrate when he was so frightened. The guards were shooting again, and they all lay flat against the ground. At first nothing happened, and he started to panic. But then he realized he could barely see the colors of the sphere, and he held it up high to catch the first rays of the sun.

The dark green began to glow. Strands of smoke spiraled away, swirling about them. Moro gasped, and Zinde stifled a cry. Jin looked up.

A hole floated before them in the air, edged in crackling darkness. Jin could see a corner of a brick wall and a view of pale blue sky and a cobbled street. A street he recognized. Heavy, cold air fell from the portal like water, flowing over their feet.

A bullet whined past. Zinde and Moro scrambled through the portal, assisted by Sir Marist, who followed them and reached back a hand to pull Jin through. They had escaped!

CHAPTER 13
THAMA

The cold was like a blow. The cobbles had ice in the cracks, and ridges of dirty snow were scattered over the roadway. Jin had forgotten the cold and how it made his feet numb. He wished he still had his coat.

Moro and Zinde, on the other hand, had never felt the cold before.

"Is-s this th-the demon w-world?" Zinde managed to say around chattering teeth.

Sir Marist took off his guard's jacket and wrapped it around her. "Looks like Albamist Street. We need to get somewhere warm, quickly. There's a police station up by Sevenbells Bridge." Jin stared at him in horror. Go to the billies? Sir Marist smiled wanly. "We are a disreputable-looking lot at the moment, especially me. I'm not sure anyone else would let us in the door."

Jin thought furiously. Sevenbells Bridge was a long way on bare feet in the cold, and Sir Marist was looking dangerously pale and ill.

"There's a...a boozing den, sir. Only a street over. If...if you won't say nothing..."

Sir Marist gave a shaky half bow. "My memory can be most adaptable, young Jin."

"And you can't talk like a nob, neither."

"Ayeh, boyo. Best drop the blowzer in the nick, likewise." Sir Marist grinned at Jin's shocked expression and tucked the rifle behind a stack of pallets with broken slats in the alley next to where they had come out. "I may have learned a few expressions from that twiddler during my lessons."

Jin realized, with a sinking feeling, it might still not work. "Um, they'll want some kind of pay. 'specially since they'll think you're in trouble with the billies." He gestured at the wounded leg.

Sir Marist reached in his trouser pocket and tossed him a few coins, one even silver. "I kept these hidden during my captivity. I thought they might come in useful for bribes."

Jin sighed. "Guess you'll do...but don't talk much and don't look at people straight-like. You look like a nob when you do that. Zinde, better hide your bracelets. Nobody flashes gold around here—not for long, anyways."

The hole back to the desert world vanished with a crackling hiss. Jin and Moro helped Sir Marist across the street and down the road, Zinde following close behind. The main door to the building Jin headed for was boarded up, but nobody but billies would try that anyway. The real door to the den was along the side and down some brick steps with an iron railing about them.

Jin went first and knocked. A rusting metal shutter slid aside and a bloodshot eye stared out.

"Whaddya want?"

Jin held up a coin. "Gotta jake needs out-of-sight for a few."

"Not likely. Go tell the brassers nobody's here."

"Like I'd help 'em—me? Jin, from the Ship and Anchor?"

The man at the window made a snarling noise, but

he did open the door. He snatched the coin from Jin's hand as they pulled Sir Marist inside.

The smell of dirt, grease, and sour beer was overwhelming, but it was warmer. With a few more coins Jin managed to get a reasonably clean cloth to tear for a bandage for Sir Marist's leg and a jug of hot mullery that was mostly water. Still, it removed the grey look from Sir Marist's face, and Zinde's teeth stopped chattering.

"A definite improvement, but we can't stay here long," Sir Marist said softly. He was sitting on a bench with his back against the wall, and watching the room. "I need you to take a message to the place I mentioned before." Jin gave him credit for not even saying the word "police" here.

"That lot don't favor folk like me," Jin pointed out. "Won't hear a word I say."

Sir Marist sighed with a tired smile. "They will if it's the right word in the right ear. Fetch me a bit of cinder from the fire."

Jin did, puzzled, and then understood when he saw Sir Marist tug an old, tattered playbill from the wall when the owner of the boozing den wasn't looking. Sir Marist quickly scribbled several lines on the back of the playbill. Jin stared at the words, wondering how he could know all the letters and yet not be able to read any of it. He had been able to read all of Mr. Andel's books.

"Give this to the one in charge, and tell him to transmit the message exactly over the station wire to the address at the bottom. It shouldn't take long after that." He smiled grimly. "Someone from...my organization will come, so wait for them and bring them here."

Someone had to go, but Jin didn't like the idea of leaving his friends in a boozing den. Sir Marist clearly expected help to come quickly, but what if the billies wouldn't even let him deliver the message?

"Maybe we should go somewhere else first," he mumbled, glancing around. There were only two other customers in the place, but that would change in a few hours when the dockworkers came off shift.

"Never fear. It's only my leg that can't function. If Miss Karestal will allow me to borrow her treasured blade, we'll do for the moment. But I'd appreciate it if you didn't stop to admire the sights on your way."

Zinde gave Sir Marist a serious look under lowered brows, but she shifted the sword from under her robes to hide under a fold of Moro's *kebba*, right next to Sir Marist's hand. Jin grimaced, but he couldn't think of a better idea.

It was still bitter cold outside, and Jin ran as fast as he could to keep warm. He kept an eye on the street, and after a while he saw what he was looking for—a hire cab going the right direction. The driver was old and fat and not paying too much attention, and the fare looked bored. Jin sprinted and lunged for the rail in the back that was used to tie down luggage, letting the motion of the cab pull him up so it didn't jerk and alert the driver.

Sneaking a lift was faster, but since he wasn't running, colder. He curled his legs up underneath himself and watched for the bridge.

There. The big torches flanking the door, indicating a station. Jin dropped off the cab, grunting with pain when his stiff legs hit the cold cobblestones. *I can't believe I'm trying to get inside a billy bin.* But he had to, and fast. It was good he had never spent much time around Sevenbells Bridge, so the billies there shouldn't know him.

He couldn't help glancing quickly over his shoulder to make sure nobody was watching before he ran up the stone steps. The door was heavy oak with a glass panel and opened only with considerable effort. Jin took a deep breath and stepped inside.

The floorboards were worn and rough, but clean. Several oil lamps hung from chains, and a potbellied iron stove put out welcome heat. Two rather surprised-looking billies were staring at him, one at a desk in the back of the room and the other at a polished wood counter. The silence lengthened, and Jin realized they were waiting for him to speak.

"Got a message for yer boss," he finally managed. His voice squeaked a little at the end, and he felt himself flush with embarrassment.

"Sure ya do," the one at the desk said, and returned his attention to the papers in front of him. The one at the counter, older and plumper, leaned over and gave Jin a closer examination.

"Message from you, lad? So important you popped out without your coat, eh? We've got no time for your games."

What would make them listen? "Nah, it were this nob, right? He gives me a penny to bring it here, an' two more if'n I get an answer back quick."

The billy at the desk looked up at that. "Money don't make a nob, rab."

"I ain't a rab! And he is a nob. Talks all them big words and sounds like they get stuck in his nose."

The counter billy laughed. "They do, that. So let's see this urgent message." He held out a large, sturdy hand.

Jin handed over the scribbled playbill reluctantly. "He said it goes to the big guy here. Got a...a wire address or sommat at the bottom. And you gotta send all the words, just like they are."

The billy at the desk got up and looked at the message with the other man.

"That don't make any sense," said the counter billy, and Jin's heart sank. Why had Sir Marist written gobbledygook, anyway?

The other billy frowned, looking at it more closely. "Hold on—that's Old Empire writing. Maybe it is from a nob. They learn that kind of thing. Useless, if you ask me." He turned and shouted at the open door in the back. "Hey, Chief!"

After a minute a billy with a fancier uniform came out. He had a stern face and grey hair and side-whiskers, and glanced at Jin with a displeased expression before frowning at the billy at the desk. "What is it now, Termain?"

Termain handed him the message. The chief frowned at it, scanning the page, then his shaggy eyebrows went up in surprise. "Who gave you this, boy?"

Jin swallowed. "Sir Janal Marist, of the Metropol. Please, sir. He's injured and needs help."

"As if the likes of them would have anything to do with this young beggar," Termain protested. "He's having you on, Chief."

The chief turned his flinty gaze to Termain. "As if the likes of him would know about the station wire, or the address for the Metropol. I recognize it. I'll send this message, lad, but it had better not be a joke or it will go hard with you. Keep him here until I get an answer," he said and left the room.

Jin shifted his feet, wondering what to do now. He'd delivered the message, but how long would it take? His bare feet, numb from the cold, were starting to burn and tingle as they warmed up.

"Why don't you come back to the fire while you wait," said the counter billy. "You look like you could use it."

"Better keep an eye on him, Josen," muttered Termain. "He'll steal you blind."

"I ain't a rab," Jin whispered as he edged past the counter and toward the stove. But Termain's objection had been mostly out of habit, it seemed, as he went back to his work and ignored Jin. Josen even offered him some hot tea in a tin cup and pointed him at a stool to sit on.

To pass the time and distract himself from worrying, Jin started reading the various papers and notices that were pinned all over the walls. Some even had pictures, usually of people's faces. There was a map of Thama pinned up, too, and there were colored pins stuck in various places. Jin got up to look at one of the notices more closely.

"See someone you recognize?" Termain was giving him a steady look.

Jin had recognized a few faces, but he wasn't about to tell a billy about it. "What's this mean? Em-bez-zel-ment," Jin sounded it out, just like Mr. Andel had taught him. Usually that helped him recognize a word, but he hadn't heard this one before.

Termain blinked. "What, you can read?"

Jin shrugged. "Most of it. I don't know that one, though."

"Well, it's...a, a kind of stealing. When someone trusts you with money, but you take it for yourself."

Termain stared at Jin. "How'd a gutter rat like you learn—"

The chief came out of the back room. He had a slightly stunned expression on his face and looked at Jin as if he found him completely baffling.

"They are coming. How badly is he hurt, lad?"

Jin started, his heart hammering. He couldn't let the billies know...embezzlement. He had done that to Mr. Andel. He'd trusted Jin, and Jin had taken the money. Ogney could split on him, and would if he knew. What was he going to do?

The billies were staring at him, and he managed to start talking again.

"He got shot in the leg. We tied it up a bit and it stopped bleeding so much, but he can't walk real good."

That got him another raised eyebrow. "Who shot him? Did you see it?"

The other billies also peppered him with questions, burning with curiosity. Jin did his best to answer without going into exactly *where* all of this had taken place, and only mentioning Zinde and Moro as his friends who had helped Sir Marist escape captivity.

Then a man burst into the station at a run, exclaiming, "Where is he? Come on, you lot, don't just stand there gaping!"

Jin wriggled past the counter and went up to him. He was a young man with yellow hair that was tousled and a coat that had been so hastily put on it had mashed half his collar underneath. He sounded like a genteel and had a fancy silk waistcoat, too.

"Are you a friend of Sir Marist?"

"Yes—you know where he is? You must be the young guide he mentioned. Lead on, the carriage is out in front."

There was a carriage, and to Jin's astonishment he was waved inside when he hesitated. Riding *in* a carriage? The young man bounded in and shut the door. "Where to?"

Jin gave him the directions, and the man shouted to the coachman. The carriage lurched and turned sharply, and Jin slid on the seat and hit the side with a grunt.

The young man grinned. "Sorry about that—we're just in an awful hurry to see him. I'm Wendel Bartly, by the bye."

"I'm Jin. Are you Metropol, too, like Sir Marist?"

Bartly nodded. "He's been missing for months, and we feared...but he's one of the clever ones. However did you find him?"

Jin shifted on the seat. "It's kinda...complicated."

"Ah, like that, is it? Well, I suppose I'll find out eventually. And we're here. Are you sure this is the right place?" Bartly looked at the boarded-up building with dismay.

Jin persuaded Bartly to wait outside while he fetched Sir Marist from the boozing den. He banged at the door, fearing he had taken too long and his friends had been attacked, but when the owner opened the door, everyone was still there. Sir Marist did have Zinde's sword in his hand, and one of the customers was holding a bleeding cut on one arm.

"In good time, Jin. You brought reinforcements, I trust?"

"Outside." Jin and Moro helped Sir Marist to stand and hobble to the door, Zinde retrieving her sword and waving it at the remaining customers as they retreated. No one in the boozing den looked willing to follow.

"Janal!" Bartly engulfed Sir Marist in a bear hug. "You look like hell!"

"I've been better," Sir Marist gasped. "Get my young friends off the street, will you? They haven't any shoes and they aren't dressed for the weather."

Bartly stared at Zinde and Moro, swathed head to foot in black robes and the guard's jacket, and his shoulders sagged. "No...no, they aren't," he said, his voice weak. "How *do* you get in these situations?"

CHAPTER 14
THE METROPOL

In the carriage, Bartly flooded the exhausted Sir Marist with question after question. Jin was on the opposite seat with Zinde and Moro, and both huddled against him with scarves tightly wrapped over their faces, shivering.

"Where are we going?" Moro whispered.

Jin shrugged. "I'm not sure. Somewhere they can take care of Sir Marist. And safer than the boozing den." And hopefully not the station, either. Jin wanted to stay well away from any billies—although he wished he'd been able to look at all the posters and see if he was on any of them. Maybe they didn't know.

Zinde shuddered. "The people there...I did not like them. I thought they would rob us."

"Probably would've. Looked like Sir Marist stopped them, though."

"It is like you said. Many buildings, and no one covers their face here. And so many people!" Moro had recovered enough to be able to look out the carriage windows, bumping his nose on the glass and jerking back. "Look, it is clear as water but hard! How strange!" He tapped the window again, looking mystified.

Zinde leaned forward to look out, too. "What are those things?"

"Zinde! *Look!* It's all water!"

She joined Moro at his window, gaping at the river as they crossed a bridge. Jin grinned and explained to the puzzled Bartly. "They've never seen that much water before."

Before they reached their destination, Jin had to explain gas lamps, the vast number of horses, dogs, a lady's fancy hat, and glass display windows for shops. He was getting more and more nervous. They were in a part of the city he had never visited, with large, ornate buildings surrounded by stone walls and iron fences. Few people were out in the cold, but those that were wore fancier clothes than Jin had ever seen —furs and silks and even, on one lady getting into a carriage, jewels.

They reminded him of the gems he'd found in the fort.

"Where are we going?" Jin asked Sir Marist.

"The Metropol headquarters, to plan our next move." He pointed. "That ancient edifice over there. Don't go wandering around, it's a complete maze. Everybody gets lost the first few weeks."

"More like a month, in my case," said Bartly, rolling his eyes.

Zinde frowned. "But you are hurt. Should you see a healer first?"

"Oh, we've got a doctor there, never fret, miss." Bartly nodded. "But we've got to move fast, if we're going to catch these villains. We can't be sure they haven't alerted their confederates here in Thama."

The carriage pulled up to a huge stone building with diamond-pane windows. A structure like a small bridge covered the entrance, and the carriage drove right underneath it. A group of people came out as soon as the carriage stopped, some with a stretcher for Sir Marist.

Jin jumped down and waved for Zinde and Moro to join him. They followed the crowd past the heavy, iron-bound oak door into a large, high-ceilinged room with a big double staircase on either side. A huge brass chandelier hung down over carpeted floors, and weapons and armor decorated the wood-paneled walls.

"Look after them, will you, Bart?" Sir Marist called as he was being carried away. "I just need a moment to get patched up."

Bartly sighed, shaking his head. "What does it take to stop that fellow? Locked up for months and shot in the bargain, and he thinks he's going to be leading the charge. Now, let's have a look at you." He gave them a thorough, considering look, running his fingers through his hair and messing it up even more. "Even if I didn't believe Janal's incredible tale, it's clear you came from a much warmer location. Let's see if I can't fix that problem, and...oy! Jofro! Swing by commissary and snag some of those sausage rolls for our guests."

Bartly herded them to a corner of the large room with several large leather sofas and waved over an older man, gesturing at Jin and his friends and speaking to him intently. Moro gazed about with wide-eyed wonder while Jin attempted to explain what was happening, which was difficult because he was confused himself. Zinde sat on the sofa, clutching her sword with one hand and running the fingers of the other over the velvet cushions scattered on the seat.

While they were getting curious glances, nobody

came to chase them out, even when Bartly wasn't there. Jin couldn't understand it. He wasn't sure about Bartly, either, until he remembered how Sir Marist treated him as a friend. Sir Marist seemed to be all right, so Bartly probably was, too.

"Ah, that's better!" Bartly returned, bearing a large platter with rolls, nuts, and roasted apples giving off tendrils of steam that smelled of cinnamon. "You were looking a little peaky, there. Eat up—we'll be moving out shortly."

"Where?" Jin asked as best he could around a mouthful of sausage roll. It was hot and flaky and had more meat than he'd seen in a long time. Moro, after a suspicious look and a careful taste, was also enthusiastically wolfing down his roll, while Zinde was trying to eat a roasted apple under her face scarf.

"Gariard—the outfit that captured Marist—owns a building near Royal Oak Park we've wanted to get a look at for some time. In fact, that's where Marist was going when he disappeared. From what he's told us, it is their main operational center for the gem trade and some of their other projects. Before now we didn't have enough proof for a writ of search, but imprisoning a government official in the course of his duty gives us the right to investigate at once."

The older man Jin had seen earlier returned, his arms piled high with a bundle of cloth.

"Given the need for haste, warmth was the first criterion," he said, depositing his burden on the sofa facing them. He picked out some thick socks and handed them to Jin, Moro, and Zinde. "Shoes were much more difficult, I am afraid, especially for the young lady."

"Don't fret, Kors! It's a raid, not a society ball."

Bartly grinned and searched the pile of clothing. "You really did ransack the far corners, didn't you? Now, where did you find this?" He held up a shawl, a deep rose color with a pattern of flowers and a fringe. "Someone has some explaining to do, I think."

Kors sighed and reached for the shawl, draping it over Zinde's shoulders. "The evidence room, sir. It had been there for some time and is unlikely to be missed."

Jin was occupied with putting on the socks, astonished to discover they didn't have a single hole. Were they new? There were boots for him and Moro, and soft leather slippers for Zinde. Everything was too big, but the thick socks helped with that.

Zinde was extremely pleased with the shawl, taking it off to examine the pattern and putting it on again. "How do I make it stay? There are no ties. If I run it will fall off."

"I see some women cross it in front and tie it behind," Jin said. "Turn around, and I'll do it for you."

By the time they were finished, the three of them looked very peculiar but were much warmer. Besides her shawl and guard's jacket, Zinde had acquired some red wool mittens and a matching muffler wrapped over her head, and Moro a very large fisherman's sweater that came down to his knees, and a tweed cap. Both still had their black scarves wrapped tightly over the lower parts of their faces.

Jin had a fur-lined hat and a boiled-wool jacket, and a dark blue muffler with white zigzags on the ends. With the fire in the hall, he was actually starting to feel too warm.

"First squad, move out!" someone shouted. Jin

noticed the room had gotten crowded, with many serious, grim-faced men. Some were checking revolvers before putting them away in coat pockets. Several moved toward the door, where a large vehicle like a baker's van had pulled up outside.

"Bartly! Where are the...oh, there they are." The one called Jofro came running toward them. "Sir Marist wants to see them. He's in the chief inspector's parlor."

Bartly sighed. "He has no business being anywhere but in bed, but it would take a dose of ether to get him there. All right, off we go." Zinde jumped off the couch, her sword clutched in her arms. He gave her a dubious look. "I'm not sure the chief inspector will be in favor of that."

"It is mine." Zinde looked at him steadily.

"What, we didn't have enough stubborn people here, and we had to import more?" Bartly threw his hands in the air. "Fine, I'll let Marist deal with it, then."

They followed Bartly out of the big room, down a carpeted hall with gaslight sconces and several doors with frosted glass panels. At the end of the hall, two double oak doors stood with brass handles and a border of carving. Bartly knocked and then opened one door.

Sir Marist was reclining on a sofa much fancier than the ones in the big room. He was still pale, but now clean and shaved and wearing clean clothes. A man in shirtsleeves with a harassed expression was packing up a leather satchel. Bloodstained bandages lay on the floor near the sofa.

"You must see it's important I go," Marist said, waving a hand sharply. "I'm the only one of us that has been in the place before."

A much older man was listening to him with an expression of polite interest, seated in an armchair and resting both of his thin hands on a silver-headed cane. He reminded Jin of Mr. Andel. Something about his eyes and how they seemed to see and understand everything.

"Your knowledge is indeed important, and even more reason we should not risk it. I commend your enthusiasm, but your health does not appear to be up to the task." If anything, the man sounded more like a nob than Sir Marist—and he was dressed like one, too.

"It isn't as if I was at death's door, sir—and I owe Jin my support during the raid, if nothing else."

Jin started, feeling nervous. What did this have to do with him?

The old man glanced at him. "You must be Jin, I'm thinking." Jin, not trusting his voice, nodded. "I am Lord Gedrin, chief inspector of Metropol. I wish to thank you and your friends for rescuing Sir Marist, at great personal risk. We are greatly in your debt. I am afraid, however, that I must ask you for your further assistance. Inexperienced as you are, you are the only jinxer we have."

Jin felt his shoulders hunch, trying to hide. There had to be seven of these Metropol brassers in the room, all of them with revolvers, and they wanted *him* to help?

"W-what can I do?"

Sir Marist struggled to sit up, wincing. "When I got in that building and started looking around, I found some areas that appeared to be completely inaccessible. No doors, no hidden panels, nothing.

They took up quite a bit of space, too. I suspect that if we want to get into those closed areas, we will need a jinxer. And I am afraid that if Mr. Karestal is in their hands, he will be in a place such as that. They would not risk him escaping."

Zinde bounced up and down, nearly dropping her sword. "I will help, too!" Moro, looking concerned, tugged on her arm, and she whispered a translation of what was being discussed.

Jin was still worried. "But I don't know how! I mean, I only sort of know how to do the doors to the other worlds. When I hold the sphere for the world I'm in, it doesn't do anything. At least not in the desert world," he added, recalling that he'd only really held the smoky green sphere long enough to get back to Thama.

"Unfortunately, we cannot advise you," said Lord Gedrin. "Sir Marist has spoken of you as brave and resourceful. Your instincts have served you well before. Trust them, and do your best."

CHAPTER 15
THE RAID ON GARIARD

Unlike the old building of the Metropol, surrounded by trees and bushes, the Gariard building was bare stone. The walls met the sidewalk and didn't even have windows on the ground floor. The windows it did have were either quite small or blocked by iron grilles painted to look like they were just windowpanes. To Jin, it looked like a building nobody could break into.

He was seated with Zinde, Moro, and Sir Marist in the back of one of the Metropol vans. The other men were already out and hiding, watching the Gariard building to make sure no one escaped. Sir Marist was shifting restlessly, either because his leg still hurt or because he wanted to be out helping.

"How are we going to get inside?" Jin asked. He kept his voice low, even though there was no way anyone could hear through the thick stone walls. "That door looks pretty strong."

Sir Marist smiled grimly. "It's stronger than it looks—the wood is just a layer over metal. We've got a breaching charge. Brace yourselves: it's going to be loud."

Two men carried a frame with a large black blob in the middle. Jin could tell it was heavy by the way they moved. A smaller, older man followed behind, crouching and striking a match. After a moment all three turned and ran, and then a gout of flame and smoke shot from the door, followed by a tremendous boom.

Their van shook and jerked, nervous whinnying coming from the horses. Zinde squeaked, and Moro grabbed the side of the van, his eyes wide.

Sir Marist peered out through the smoke. "Steady...ah, that's done it! They're pulling the door free with hooks now."

Jin watched the twisted metal fall to the pavement with a crash. Several men, guns drawn, ran through the door, and shortly after that came the sound of gunshots.

"I've got to see what's going on." Sir Marist reached for his crutch, but Zinde kicked it away.

"They said for you to stay until they came back," she said, putting both hands on the hilt of her sword, point resting on the floor, and glaring at him. "Do you want to be shot in *both* legs?"

"Is he really trying to go in there now?" Moro asked in Rabani.

"Yes, because he is stupid."

Moro picked up the crutch, placing it out of Sir Marist's reach. "See Zinde Karestal, daughter with poor judgment, saying *you* act unwisely. You are truly scolded." He shook his head, grinning. Zinde kicked him in the shin.

Sir Marist gave Zinde a dubious glance when she translated, but when Jin nodded, stifling his laughter, he just groaned and sank his face in his hands.

"What did I ever do to deserve you three? I may as well be back in my cell in the fort."

"There are people coming out." Jin pointed, hoping to distract him. The first group he did not recognize, and they had their hands bound behind their backs. Some of the Metropol followed, lining the prisoners up on the far side of the street.

Sir Marist frowned, watching. "That's not very many. I expected Gariard to have more people here."

A blond man with a revolver still in his hand came outside—Bartly. He came over to their van, his face grim. Jin started to worry. From what he had seen, Bartly laughed at everything.

"A bit of a development, Marist. Someone got out. We need to search the whole place immediately, before Tomas finds out and tells all his friends at court how rude we are."

"Blast!" Sir Marist clenched his hands on his knees. "I thought you had the place surrounded."

"I did. If my men can be believed, the fellow literally came out of the wall. No door there, hidden or otherwise. They tried to catch him, but he was too far away." Bartly glanced away, grimacing, then looked at Jin. "We need you now. You'd best stay here, Janal. They're still fighting."

"If you are going to put a young boy in danger, you can bloody well have me, too," Sir Marist snapped. "I can be of use guarding him, if nothing else. And it's not like we'll be racing in pursuit for miles in a building, so I won't be holding you back. Show some sense, Bart!"

Bartly glowered at him. "If anything happens to you or the boy, Gedrin will be *displeased* at me, and at length."

"Then you had better take care nothing happens to us. Now help me down."

Bartly continued to grumble and complain. Jin followed Sir Marist out of the van, both scared and excited to see what would happen. While he wasn't paying attention, Zinde scrambled down, too.

"You don't need to go," Jin said.

"I can help protect you, too, just like him." Zinde pointed her sword at Sir Marist. "You are helping my family, so I should. Also it is cold, and I do not want to wait in this cart."

Jin looked up at Moro. "Do you want to come, too? There is still fighting, they say."

"No," Moro said frankly. "But Zinde will go whether we let her or not, and someone needs to keep an eye on her. You will be doing your magic, and you do not know her as I do. You trust her too much."

Zinde gasped, her eyes wide with outrage. "And yet you have trusted me many times! Did I not help you when your donkey escaped and ate the headman's melons? And no one ever found out!"

"Until now." Moro tilted his head at Jin.

Zinde waved an impatient hand. "Jinli is our friend! He keeps secrets."

Jin nodded, fighting to keep from grinning. "I won't tell anyone. Come, they wait for us."

Bartly was, in fact, waving at them frantically. "We don't have much time. Tomas lives close by, and he's bound to cause all kinds of trouble to keep us from his secrets. So, young Jin, if you could find these secrets before he gets here, it would be greatly appreciated."

"Who is this Tomas?" Jin asked.

"The man who owns Gariard," Sir Marist said, gasping as he hobbled across the street. "Very, very wealthy. Very, very powerful, and with many powerful friends. We had to be careful moving against him. I was trying to find proof when I was captured. My word alone was enough to allow us to search his building, but we will need more to convict him of his crimes. Hence the speed of this raid. He'll hide the evidence given half a chance."

Once they passed the scorched and blown-out door, the inside of the Gariard building was very different from the old wood and leather furnishings of the Metropol. The walls were covered with pale gold patterned wallpaper and white trim that looked like it had been smeared with gold. Even the rich carpets were cream with gold designs. It was easy to see where the Metropol men had gone, since they left sooty footprints behind.

Jin and his friends followed Bartly, with Sir Marist limping behind on his crutch. The rooms they passed were empty save for white and gold-smeared furniture. They mostly looked like fancy parlors.

"As Sir Marist warned us, the entire interior of the building is sealed off," Bartly said, waving his hands as they turned a corner. "All those open rooms are on the exterior walls, with windows. All we see on the other side of the hallway is solid wall, and it goes up several stories. Oh, and down to the cellar. We found a few small openings for the furnace, and what we think are ventilators, but nothing else. And then we found this."

He gestured, and Jin stared in befuddlement. The hallway widened here, and a broad sweep of steps went up about six feet—and just stopped against the wall. There were no doors, and no sign there ever had been any doors.

"This place doesn't make any sense," Jin complained. Zinde and Moro were staying close to him, looking about with wondering expressions. "Why have all these stairs if they don't go anywhere useful?"

Zinde cast a suspicious glance at the stairs. "Who knows why the *maahtik* do anything?"

"The *maahtik* are evil, not stupid." Moro folded his arms, standing before the stairs and studying them. He got down on his knees and stared even more closely.

"What are you doing? We need to find a way inside, not take naps!"

Moro smiled. "I think instead of talk. Someone named Zinde should try it. See, the carpet is worn down a little in the center. People have walked on it here."

"Oh, a hidden door?" Zinde had her sword in her hands, looking like she was ready to beat down the wall.

"We already tried that," Bartly said, correctly interpreting her actions. "Well, we shot at it. Seems to be solid stone." He pointed to some pockmarks on the wall.

"Then they must use portals somehow. Well, we thought as much." Sir Marist sat down on a chair with a grimace. "Well, Jin? What do you think?"

Jin swallowed hard. With a sinking feeling, he realized everybody was looking at him. *I don't know how I do any of this. How do they expect me to figure it out?* But they did, and he had to, somehow. Quickly. If he didn't, Zinde's father wouldn't be rescued. And now that he thought about it, Zinde and Moro couldn't go back to the village, either. The fort people would be looking for them back in Darha. He had to find a way to open up the hidden area and stop Gariard or his friends would be trapped here in Thama.

He dug in his pocket for the two crystal spheres. Maybe they'd give him an idea. Jin only glanced at the golden one, but it was enough to start it glowing, and he quickly closed his hand around it. They didn't need to go back to Darha, and he didn't know what would be waiting for them there.

The green sphere did not glow. He stared at it anyway, studying the swirls of smoke that twined inside. Did they move?

Then Jin remembered how he had felt the sphere warm when it got near others, in the vault room of the fort. Perhaps he needed to touch the hidden portal or doorway to get through. He went up the stairs and trailed his fingers over the wall, but he felt nothing other than the rough surface of the wallpaper.

Zinde came up the stairs to join him and squinted hard at the wall, as if she could see the way in by sheer effort.

"Maybe you should try a different spot, Jinli. Besides, the people inside will expect someone to come in from here. To take them by surprise, we should go a different way."

"She is right." Jin turned and stared at Moro in astonishment, and so did Zinde. Moro grinned. "It can happen."

Jin tugged on Zinde's arm before she could kick Moro in the shin again. "Come on, let's keep looking."

Loud voices came from the far end of the hall, near the entrance door. They were getting louder. Now Jin could see a group of Metropol men trying to stop a stranger in a large dark coat from coming forward.

"Where is this alleged writ you speak of? Who is in charge of this outrage?" The stranger pushed through the men, heading straight for Sir Marist and Bartly.

"Well, that didn't take long," Sir Marist murmured.

Bartly narrowed his eyes. "I am in charge of this investigation. Who are you, sir, and why do you interfere with it?"

"I am Mr. Wilest, Mr. Tomas's legal representative. Produce your writ of search or leave immediately!" Bartly silently handed the man a folded paper, which he read intently. "This document only permits you to search the premises for evidence. It does *not* allow you to damage anything. You will be sent a bill for the door you destroyed as well as any other damage we find."

"No one opened when we knocked," Sir Marist said dryly.

Mr. Wilest glared at him. "This is not a joking matter! Anyone could wander in off the street...like these thieving children! What are they doing here? Remove them immediately!"

Jin heard Zinde's gasp and stepped on her foot quickly. "Ay! You gabbers pay'n whats promised first!"

Sir Marist's eyes brightened with comprehension. "Yes, Bartly, pay the lad his penny and see him out, do."

Grabbing Zinde by the wrist, Jin tugged her away and down the hall. "We hide and search," he said in Rabani. She glared at him but didn't say anything, to his great relief. Moro followed behind, his expression a careful blank.

Bartly looked discreetly over his shoulder. "He's

arguing with Sir Marist and looking the other way. Off you go, and be careful! We'll keep him busy as long as we can."

Jin ran down the side corridor that Bartly indicated. He saw a staircase and headed down. Anyplace was better than where he was now.

"That man called us thieves!" Zinde hissed in a whisper. "You let him think this!"

Jin hunched his shoulders. "We had to get away. Sir Marist and Bartly knew what we were doing. Now we can try and find a way in and that man won't know." He couldn't know about Jin, could he? Jin had never seen Mr. Wilest before, but that didn't mean anything.

"But he insulted us!"

"Don't be so loud. The *maahtik* are still here somewhere." Jin turned away, unable to face her accusing gaze and feeling angry. *I had to do it. Mr. Andel wanted it that way.*

The hallway at the bottom of the stair was empty and much more plain than the one upstairs. They walked silently to the far end. The walls were painted instead of wallpapered and had only a few decorations. One was a painting of a sailing ship, hanging over a large wooden cabinet. Moro went over to look at it, and Zinde joined him. They both looked puzzled.

"What is it?"

"It's for going across water. Lots of water, like an ocean."

"How does it stay up on the water?"

"I think because it has air inside, like a reed." Jin ran his hand over the wall while clutching the sphere. Just like before, he felt nothing. What was he going to do if he couldn't figure out a way in?

"Where does all this water *come* from?" Moro sounded completely bewildered. "Did this world get all of it? You must not need any well diggers at all."

"I don't know. It was always there. This water you can't drink. It is salty."

"How can that be possible?" Moro leaned closer to study the painting. "Is it true?"

Jin realized he hadn't actually seen the ocean himself, or tasted the water. He'd just heard stories. He opened his mouth to say so, but then he felt something odd. The sphere in his hand was humming.

The vibration was getting stronger, and he could see a pale light growing in the center of the sphere. He held it up and noticed the light was brighter one direction, so he moved that way. It just felt right.

Jin looked up and froze in astonishment. A man's head was sticking out of the wall, looking cautiously about from a glowing portal. He was looking away from them, and Jin quickly hid behind the cabinet, pulling Zinde and Moro behind him before they were seen.

The man pulled back. Voices came from the portal, hushed and worried. A different person scrambled out of the portal, in shirtsleeves and vest. His eyes were wide with fright, and sweat trickled down his face, and as soon as his feet touched the ground, he ran for the stairs.

Jin felt his heart beating faster and huddled closer to the cabinet. Zinde had her sword clutched in her hand, and for once he was glad. The Gariard jinxers had helped him without realizing it. They knew how to open the portal, and maybe he could figure it out for himself now. He peeked around the edge of the cabinet.

Moro shifted. "What are you going to do?" he whispered.

"The portal is staying open. I wonder why? Maybe we can sneak in..."

The sound of running footsteps came down the stairs, and the same man in shirtsleeves flung himself back through the portal.

"Metropol is still there, but Wilest is, too. The message got through."

"Good! We'll wait an hour or so before—"

The portal closed, and the voices cut off.

Jin sagged against the wall, suddenly feeling tired. He'd been tired before or he wouldn't have thought about trying to get in the portal opened by Gariard. But it wasn't very smart to open a portal anywhere if he didn't know what was on the other side.

But could he? Opening a portal on the same world felt different than between worlds. It didn't have the same kind of raw power to it. Maybe if he just started that same feeling all by himself, it would work.

Jin got up, picked up the green sphere, and concentrated. It was harder than he thought. The feeling kept slipping away when he concentrated on it. It was a humming feeling that he remembered, so Jin started humming himself.

No, not quite like that. A little deeper, like a rumble. He changed his humming, and suddenly it clicked. He felt the sphere vibrate and the light inside started to grow.

The crinkly, dark edges of the portal began to appear on the wall. Quickly, heart pounding, Jin dropped the sphere, and the portal vanished.

Zinde wrinkled her brow. "Why did you stop?"

"What if there are Gariard people with guns on the other side?"

Moro got to his feet. "Can you make the hole smaller? The one they made was not as big as the one you did when we escaped."

Jin blinked. "I don't know. I haven't tried that."

"If the hole is small, and closer to the ground, they may not see it. Then you can look and decide if it is safe to open wider."

Jin gaped at him, and Moro grinned.

"Once or twice in his ancient life, this Moro is clever," Zinde said. "Try it, Jinli!"

The trick was to not open the portal completely, so the people inside could see it. It was easier to make the portal low than to make it small, but after a few attempts Jin started to get a feel for it. He was glad he'd tested it when he made his first real attempt. Although the portal was under a table, the room was brightly lit, and he could see the feet of at least ten people.

"I can't see," Zinde whispered. Jin shifted over a bit. "Look, over there. A room with a door."

They guessed the distance wrong the first time, but the next try worked. The small portal showed nothing but darkness, and even when Zinde put her ear to the portal, she could hear nothing but faint voices from the other side of the door. Jin slowly widened the portal.

As light from the hallway came through, they could see more of the room. At first all Jin could see were walls completely covered with metal cabinets and drawers. They looked familiar, and Jin blinked when he realized why. They looked like the room under the fort, where they had found the spheres.

Then Moro grabbed his arm. The light now showed a man sitting in a chair, his head bowed. Jin felt a jolt of fear, but before he could close the portal, Zinde gasped and leaped through. Dropping the sword, her hands tore at the gag in the man's mouth as she tried to stifle sobs.

"Aba, Aba! I found you!"

CHAPTER 16
THE GREATEST TREASURE

Moro had to help cut the ropes binding Zinde's father, but then Mr. Karestal was free and through the portal, blinking at the light. He held on to Zinde as if he was afraid she would disappear.

Now that Jin could see him better, Mr. Karestal had an interesting appearance. His clothing was Caerda and his hair was cut that way, too. It went oddly with his brown skin and strong resemblance to Zinde, and it was jarring to see him without the desert robes or the black scarf covering his lower face. He wore a neatly trimmed beard with traces of grey in it, and his face was haggard and worn.

Now that his arms were free, he was hugging his daughter tightly while she excitedly whispered all of their adventures.

"Oho!" Moro punched Jin in the arm, grinning. "See if their faces are not shown to you now! Why does he wear the strange clothing of the *maahtik*?"

"They said...they said I must serve them here, as in the *maaht*, or they would harm my family." Mr. Karestal closed his eyes, shuddering. "I could find no way out. What else could I do?" He got a better look at Jin, and blinked. "But you are..."

"He found you, Aba! He is a magician, and a friend. He just looks like a *maahtik*."

Mr. Karestal nodded, looking a little dazed. Moro,

who had been carefully keeping his gaze averted, handed him his face scarf.

"No...shall you uncover your face to cover mine?"

Still feeling he was missing something, Jin unwrapped his muffler. "Will this work? It's too warm in here, anyway."

All of the Rabani were relieved and pleased at his suggestion. Mr. Karestal appeared much more comfortable with his scarf in place. Jin supposed it must be like going out without your shirt to them. Not decent.

"I guess we should tell them we know how to get in now," Jin said. "But how can we do that while Mr. Wilest is there watching?"

Zinde turned, still holding on to her father's arm. "Outside there are many of these Metropol, yes? We send one of them in."

Moro rolled his eyes. "Yes, and it is the same difficulty. How do we go outside without being seen? Or they come to us here?"

Zinde had a very smug expression in her eyes. "See Jinli, to whom walls are as smoke. That much is easy!"

It wasn't exactly easy—they first had to find a wall where only Metropol men were watching—but soon Zinde had escaped the building and sent the message, and within minutes Sir Marist and Bartly had stepped through the outside portal with her.

"Oh, this is very clever," Sir Marist approved. "And Mr. Wilest is completely oblivious we can enter at will. Karestal! It is a profound relief to see you alive and well."

Mr. Karestal's eyes widened. "*zin*-Marist, of course you would be here! I feared you had been captured.

But...you are hurt?"

Sir Marist grimaced. "I was captured, all right. They had me locked up in the fort, and I was shot during the escape. Your daughter and her friends found me while looking for you. Why did Gariard have you tied up?"

Mr. Karestal shook his head, hugging Zinde again. "They feared I would aid their attackers—I did not know it was you. I had no way to escape. Only their magicians can open the portals."

"And Jinli!" Zinde pointed to Jin, looking proud. "He figured it out. He can do anything the *maahtik* can!"

"Sometimes," Jin mumbled, feeling his face heat.

"Looks like we can get that evidence now." Bartly rubbed his hands in a satisfied manner, a mischievous grin on his face. "I'll have the others come in the same way, then. Perhaps I can get Wilest to go away, since it will look like we are leaving."

"If he doesn't, make sure he can't get to this floor. Have them bring the wagons around, and block the street," Sir Marist said. "And don't forget the Gariard people don't need doors or windows to get out, so keep the guard in place all around the building."

Bartly made a face at him and stepped out of the portal again.

Sir Marist looked at Jin, lifting an eyebrow. "We've been keeping you busy—can you keep going a while longer? Does it tire you to do so many portals?"

Jin ducked his head. "A bit. Keeping 'em open gets hard. But these ones in the walls aren't too bad."

"Close it, then. It will take Bartly a few minutes to assemble the troops, and you can rest." He turned to Mr. Karestal. "Now, sir, we need your advice. It would be best not to let our adversary know how much we have discovered. Gariard's legal advisor is in the building, and they've got jinxers like Jin able to escape this walled-up section. How can we capture the people inside without them getting loose?"

Mr. Karestal rubbed his forehead. "The magicians —you call them jinxers? To open these portals, they must have keys. Like a gem of great price. They can make them glow with light. Yes, yes, like that!" He pointed to the crystal sphere Jin held up. "But they are not permitted to keep these keys and use them as they wish. The supervisor keeps them in his safe until the keys are needed."

"Right, then." Sir Marist glanced down the bare hallway. "Where is this office? Can we get in without raising the alarm? It's not like we have to open the safe to prevent them from using the spheres."

"The office is the room next to the vault, where I was. But to be sure of success, you must open the safe." Mr. Karestal raised a warning finger. "I only know their usual practice. In a time of danger, the supervisor might well keep the key on his person to have it ready at a moment's notice. If you open the case and one is missing, then you will know that is what he has done. If all are present, they cannot escape you."

Sir Marist made a face. "I had hoped to avoid opening the safe...if we can't blow it open, it will take time, and that risks discovery. Well, I suppose we should get started. Ready, Jin? One more wall, if you've rested enough."

Jin went over to where he thought the next room would be. Something Sir Marist had said was making him think...with the sphere, *any* wall could have a portal. And it didn't really matter how thick it was, either. It felt a little different, maybe it needed more pushing with his magic, but he could do it. And that gave him an idea.

"Where is the safe in this supervisor's room?" he asked.

"I can draw for you, if—ah, thank you." One of the Metropol men handed Mr. Karestal a torn piece of paper and the stub of a pencil. Mr. Karestal quickly outlined the plan of the room. "The door is here, and the safe is in this corner. It is large, as large as you," he added, the corners of his eyes crinkling in a smile.

Sir Marist was watching with interest. "What are you thinking, Jin?"

"Ah! I see!" Zinde bounced up and down with excitement. "It is next to the wall of the hallway, and Jinli can reach inside with his magic and none of the *maahtik* will know!"

"Oh my. So he can." Sir Marist shook his head. "I am still not quite used to what jinxers can accomplish."

Jin held up the sphere and focused. It took more effort this time, either because he was getting so tired he could barely stand or because the iron of the safe was more difficult to make a portal in than the stone of the wall. But slowly, surely, the portal opened to shelves and the gleaming metal mechanisms of the safe door behind them.

"Quick, grab everything you see—we'll sort it out later. I suppose this is the case you referred to, Karestal?"

Sir Marist held a leather-covered case, about the size of a large book. He opened it. Inside were eight crystal spheres, each in a special compartment. Three were the smoky green for Galetan, this world, one was the fiery gold of Darha, and the others Jin had never seen before—pale, clear blue with swirls of bubbles; a riot of flecks of bright color; deep midnight blue with crystal drops that glowed; and what looked like pearl except it was not white, but blue and green and purple.

"Excellent! None are missing. What else did we find?"

Moro held up a thick book, bound in red. Zinde had a bundle of letters, tied up with a green ribbon.

"Just some boring banknotes. It's only a few hundred thousand royals," Bartly said dryly. "I do hope nobody but us ever learns of this little trick. If thieves learn how to do this, we'll never be able to stop them."

Jin started so badly he dropped the sphere. Terrified, he darted a look at Bartly—but Bartly wasn't even looking at him. His heart was hammering as he picked up the crystal sphere. This was going to be even worse than the billies had been about him finding things to sell. How could he prove he wasn't a thief if something disappeared?

"Everyone ready, then? You take a squad up to the next floor once we're in, Bart, and I—"

"—will be staying here, *outside* the sealed section only a jinxer can get to, or I will personally carry you out, and yes I could, because you barely have the strength to stand up right now, and furthermore, if I hear any more argument I will deputize the young lady to give you a beating for disobeying Lord Gedrin's orders." Bartly glared at Sir Marist, then turned to Jin. "Now, how about a door, Jin?"

"She probably would, too," Sir Marist muttered as

Jin let the crowd of Metropol men into the supervisor's office. Zinde looked at him and then at Jin, but she didn't say anything. Her eyes were somber.

The room beyond the portal was in shadow, the only light coming from the pane of glass over the door. Jin could hear voices beyond the door. They sounded angry.

One of the Metropol men carefully climbed through the portal and into the dark room, crawling on the floor. Reaching the door, he grasped the doorknob and turned it.

"Good, it's unlocked," murmured Sir Marist.

More men climbed through the portal. Then one yanked the door open, a whistle shrilled, and a voice shouted, "Hands in the air! Metropol!"

CHAPTER 17
CONFESSIONS

Jin's memories of the rest of the night were confused and muddled. Once all the Gariard people had been captured, Bartly had sent him, Sir Marist, and the Rabani back to the Metropol building. He remembered a carriage, even larger and more comfortable than the first one. The leather seats were quilted and amazingly soft, and a deep red. Moro and Zinde pointed out interesting sights for Mr. Karestal's information as they went, explaining them as if they had always known what they were.

There was something about jewels and a thick red book—or had that been earlier? Sir Marist fell asleep and had to be carried out once they arrived, and when the prisoners showed up, Bartly wanted Jin and his friends out of sight. The Metropol people were still worried about Mr. Tomas.

"You're all valuable witnesses," Bartly had said. "You stay here in the library until it's safe. Tomas will be getting desperate now, and he was dangerous enough before. No telling what he'd do to keep you quiet."

A library, it turned out, was an entire *room* full of books. And big, comfortable leather chairs, and tables with brass lamps with green glass shades. Even though he was so tired he could barely keep his eyes open, Jin felt a sudden pang he couldn't tell Mr.

Andel about this room. So many books...

Jin collapsed in one of the chairs and immediately fell asleep, but he kept waking up in a sweat of fear, his heart pounding. Sir Marist had said Metropol was just like the billies, and now he'd seen it for himself. They arrested people who committed crimes and took them away. Sir Marist didn't seem like a billy, but he wasn't there now and Jin wasn't sure if he'd be coming back.

His first instinct was to run away and hide in the corners of Thama he knew better than anyone. But that would mean Moro and Zinde and her father would not be able to return to Darha. Then he thought about all of them escaping, but there had been too many people about, and even wondering about making a portal somewhere made his head hurt. Then he would fall asleep again. Sometimes he dreamed of prisons and chains, and sometimes of the strange crystal spheres they'd found in the safe. What did they do?

The next time he woke, Jin didn't feel drowsy again, possibly because he'd gotten a crick in his neck from sleeping in the leather chair. He looked about the room, still lit dimly by the green lamps. Mr. Karestal was snoring softly on a couch, holding Zinde in his arms. She was still wearing the flowery shawl tied about her.

Moro had ignored the furniture and was lying in front of the fireplace on a thick rug. Rubbing his stiff neck, Jin decided Moro had probably made the right choice.

It was quiet now, no voices outside. Jin got up and very slowly opened the library door, easing it closed again when he saw someone standing in front of it.

So, they weren't locked in, but they were being guarded.

If he was going to run away, now was the best time. Jin went and crouched by Moro, shaking his shoulder.

"Wake up, ancient grandfather!" he whispered.

Moro stretched and yawned, opening one eye to glare at Jin. "Rude infant. Respect the wisdom of your elders and follow their example by sleeping."

"Don't make so much noise! I need to talk to you."

Moro got up, grumbling under his breath, and followed Jin to the far corner of the library, away from Mr. Karestal and Zinde. "When you wake people, it is polite to have food for them." He sat down cross-legged and yawned again.

Jin sat down next to him. "I want us all to go back to Darha, right away."

Moro blinked, opening his eyes wide. "I am glad, but why now? Before breakfast?"

"There is trouble for me here." Jin shifted uncomfortably. "And I don't know any of these people except for Sir Marist."

The trouble was, Jin didn't really want to leave Thama forever. Coming back, all the little things he'd forgotten seemed wonderful to him. Comfortable. Where everyone spoke the language he knew, and everything wasn't always strange and different. He liked Darha a lot, but he liked Galetan, too.

He also wanted to show his friends things, like the Summer Fair by the river, and the man with the trained squirrel, and the cranes that lifted cargo out of the ships at the docks. He especially wanted to see Moro get rained on, just to see his face when it happened.

If he was in prison, though, he couldn't do that.

Moro thought for a moment. "Have they said we may not leave? I do not understand their words. Why would they wish us to stay?"

"They wish us to speak to their elders, to tell them what the *maahtik* have done."

Jin and Moro looked up sharply. Zinde was standing there, rubbing her eyes. She sat down next to them with her usual floating grace.

"Jinli, what is wrong? Share your troubles with your friends so they are lessened."

"Yes." Moro nodded. "What do you fear?"

Jin hunched his shoulders, trying to think what would be safe to tell them. "I have enemies here. If they find out...if they come here and accuse me to the Metropol, they might take me away."

Moro smiled. "Bah! You helped these Metropol catch *their* enemies. They will not listen to anyone who speaks against you."

"It doesn't matter what they want to do. They have to follow the law."

Zinde wasn't speaking, just looking at Jin with a serious expression in her dark eyes. Then she shifted. "I will help you, Jinli. My father is found safe. Know that my debt to you is so big it cannot be measured." She took a deep breath, swallowing, before continuing in Caerda, "I saw your eyes, when there was talk of thieves in the stone building. Are you a thief, Jinli?"

Jin wrapped his arms around his knees, hugging them and feeling his throat tighten. Hearing Zinde ask the question didn't upset him nearly as much as hearing her ask in a language Moro didn't understand

—so he wouldn't know. Moro knew something was wrong and was glancing back and forth with worried eyes, but he didn't *know*.

"I used to be," he whispered, keeping his eyes on the floor. "Food, mostly. I would get so hungry...but Mr. Andel made me promise not to do it anymore. And I haven't, not for years now. I mean, sometimes I would take his money if he told me to, to get things for him when he was sick. Only if he told me to." Jin met Zinde's eyes. "And I never took anything when I was in Darha. Well, I suppose I took things from Goront's office..." He wasn't going to tell her about embezzlement. He just wasn't.

Zinde waved her hand. "So did I. That's not stealing, we were rescuing my father." She sounded greatly relieved. Switching back to Rabani, she continued, "so these enemies would say you had stolen something, and the Metropol would have to listen. No, we don't want that. But I do not think my father will agree to leave now. He wishes to help Sir Marist."

"How long will that take?" Moro asked. "My father will be worried when I do not return. He will think the *maahtik* have taken me."

Jin grinned at him. "They did!" Moro punched him in the arm.

"Stop that!" Zinde glared at him. "So, we can't leave now. Hear my thoughts. I believe Sir Marist is a friend and will help us if he can. Your enemies may not find you before we are done here, Jin. If they do, Sir Marist may be able to stop them. If not, you must always keep your magic close to your hand and be ready to escape. Even if my father and I and Moro are trapped, if you are free, you can rescue us and take us home. Do not forget, I still have the magics we took from the *maaht*. Even if they take yours, we can leave."

"That is a good plan." Moro stopped, looking puzzled. "You are getting better at plans, Zinde. Are you ill?"

Zinde punched him in the arm.

The faint snores coming from the distant sofa changed to snorts, then the sound of Mr. Karestal turning over. After a moment the snores returned, and the children relaxed.

"Stop making so much noise! He'll wake up!"

Moro flapped his hand at her. "If you didn't hit me so hard, I wouldn't scream."

"If you didn't say things that make her hit you, she wouldn't," Jin pointed out, stifling a laugh.

"True, but...Zinde. Do not hit me. I only wonder, what will your father do when he returns? He cannot be seen by the *maahtik*, just like Jinli. And I do not think he would like digging wells."

Jin blinked. He hadn't thought about it, but the people in the fort were trapped there. They had taken the extra spheres to prevent them from chasing Sir Marist when they escaped, but the *maahtik* still had their weapons and controlled Gilbadeh. And if he went back now, he'd have to hide, too.

The door to the library opened, and Sir Marist hobbled in on his crutch. He was looking much better than he had the previous night, and he had a small smile on his face like he was looking forward to something.

"Ah, good, you're all still here. Would anyone care for some breakfast?"

CHAPTER 18
LAW AND HONOR

Sir Marist led them on a roundabout path through the Metropol building involving multiple passageways, halls, and a set of stairs that he had to hop up on one foot. They were going to the commissary, which Jin had heard mentioned before, connected with food. He wasn't sure what to expect, but he discovered it was a large room with tables and chairs and a row of large pots and dishes ranged along one wall, full of food. The smells made Jin's mouth water. Zinde made Sir Marist sit down, and Jin and Moro gathered up food for everyone.

They were all hungry, especially Mr. Karestal, who hadn't had anything to eat all yesterday. Jin discovered some sausages, and Moro was trying to figure out a meat pie. Sir Marist kept looking at his watch while he ate.

"What's wrong?" Jin finally asked.

"Lord Gedrin is bringing in Mr. Tomas this morning, and I expected to hear something by now. I hope nothing has gone wrong." Sir Marist flicked his watch closed and put it back in his vest pocket. "He asked that we all be prepared to come to his office—especially you, Jin."

"Me?" Jin swallowed a bit of sausage wrong and coughed until Moro pounded him on the back. "What about me?"

"We're going to need your help for a while yet, I imagine. Gariard has other buildings, which might well have sealed areas...and having a jinxer available would be convenient." Sir Marist turned. "Ah, we're being summoned."

The man that had found them warm clothing, Kors, was standing in the door of the commissary.

"We'd like you all to stay in the back for the moment," Kors said on the way to Lord Gedrin's office. "Mr. Tomas doesn't know you have returned or that we were able to successfully search his building."

The large office was crowded. Jin and the others edged up against the wall, near a window but still out of sight of the center of the room. Lord Gedrin was seated at his desk, and Bartly stood next to him with one arm in a sling and a bandaged hand. Standing before him was a tall man with light brown hair flowing to his shoulders, and wearing a dark blue silk jacket. The tall man was speaking in a loud, angry voice.

"Your summons is a grave offense. It is an insult for a gentleman like myself to be treated in such a way. You will release me at once!"

"Are you forgetting we have a writ of search for your place of business? Someone connected with Gariard abducted one of my agents in the performance of his duties. We have every right to investigate," Lord Gedrin said mildly.

"If any of my employees has committed a crime, naturally you must investigate. But you have ransacked and exploded my place of business for no cause! You have no evidence of any other wrongdoing. It is not illegal to protect our private matters. Of course I keep the transformational secrets of our jinxers concealed. It is our trade secret." So, this must be the Mr. Tomas who was in charge of Gariard.

"You claim you have not been, in reality, selling gems you have mined elsewhere?"

Mr. Tomas's face turned red. "Absolute nonsense! Everyone knows jinxers transform our gems. Why would we need to mine something we create ourselves? More to the point, not a single ship has ever carried our cargo to Thama. We create everything here."

Lord Gedrin gestured, and two men carried a small wooden chest in front of his desk and opened it. Peering through gaps in the crowd, Jin saw it was full of the fiery gems—and on top of the gems was a familiar leather-covered box.

"The supervisor threw the keys to the vault into the furnace," Sir Marist murmured to Jin. "Bartly tried to rescue them, but it was too late. Fortunately I had brought my twiddler's tools for just such an occasion, and we were able to open enough of the vault to get some of the contents."

"Where did you get those?" Mr. Tomas shouted. "Only Gariard has these gems in such quantities."

"Are you certain? One gem looks very much like another, after all." Lord Gedrin seemed completely calm, maybe even a little bored. Sir Marist, on the other hand, was watching the scene with fascination.

"I am completely certain. That case is also Gariard property and should never have left...that is, should be returned immediately. It can have no possible connection to this alleged abduction complaint you mention."

"Are you prepared to swear to it, Mr. Tomas? Here is a statement for you to sign to that effect. You understand, for property of that value we must be sure of the owner before returning it."

"Yes, yes! I am quite willing to sign." Mr. Tomas took the pen Lord Gedrin was offering and scribbled on the paper. He returned the pen and immediately picked up the leather case. It seemed to Jin that his hands were trembling.

Jin realized another man was standing against the wall near them, in the shadows cast by the window draperies. He was watching Tomas intently, and Jin felt a sudden chill of fear. This man looked dangerous. He had deep-set, dark eyes and a nose like a hawk. His clothing wasn't fancy, but it seemed rich anyway, and he wore a large carved gold ring on one hand.

The man glanced at Jin, and one eyebrow curved up. Jin just stared, not daring to move, and then he heard a sharp, indrawn breath from Sir Marist, behind him. When he looked back, Sir Marist was staring wide-eyed, face pale, at the stranger. He started to bow, but the stranger smiled slightly and held up his hand to stop him.

Now Jin was completely confused. What would make Sir Marist react like that—and who would a nob bow to?

Another, bigger nob. Jin squeezed his eyes shut and wondered how fast he could open a portal.

"I will send my people with an armored carriage to remove my property," Mr. Tomas said. "I trust you will keep this under guard until they arrive?"

"One moment." Lord Gedrin's gaze was no longer gentle and bored. He looked almost as dangerous as the nob in the shadows now. "You have signed a statement claiming this property as yours, specifically identified. It was found in a safe in your place of business—along with this." He placed the red book on his desk. "A ledger, Mr. Tomas. A ledger with some very curious entries. If you have no mine, why do you require so much mining equipment? Very expensive mining equipment, it appears."

Mr. Tomas had gone very pale. He licked his lips. "It is not a crime to purchase mining equipment. And again, I fail to see what possible connection this has to a purported abduction—always assuming such an abduction took place."

Lord Gedrin looked over at Sir Marist. "Would you care to address that issue?"

"I was most certainly abducted, and by force, even after I had identified myself as an agent of Metropol. I believe I recognized some of my captors during the recent removal of prisoners from the Gariard building." Sir Marist smiled at Mr. Tomas's expression of fury. "Oh, and I was not their only prisoner."

He nodded at Mr. Karestal, who stepped forward. Mr. Tomas snapped his head around. When he saw Mr. Karestal, Tomas clenched his fists but said nothing.

Lord Gedrin steepled his fingers. "Do you recognize this man?"

"Yes. He is the one who gives orders for Gariard. I saw him many times after I was captured."

"How did you come to this place?"

"His men caught me. They took me through the hole in the air and told me I would never leave. That I would never see my world or my family again. When

Metropol came, his men tied me up and said if the walls were breached, they would kill me."

"He is a lying foreigner! Why would you believe him before me?"

Sir Marist spoke. "Because I am not a foreigner but a Metropol officer, and I say the same thing. I know this man, and I met him in his home world. Because he aided me, Gariard imprisoned him and threatened his family."

Mr. Tomas was shaking now, but Jin couldn't tell if it was from anger or fear. "You must have subverted one of my people," he snarled. "It's the only way...but I will deal with them later. Again, you have nothing but assertion. His word against mine. Home world? What other world is there but this one? *Where is your proof?*"

Jin already had the fiery crystal sphere in his hand, the one that had first opened the world of jinxers for him, when Sir Marist said, "Let's have a portal, Jin."

The dark, crackling shadow appeared in midair and exploded open. Jin was angry. This Tomas was behind all the bad things that had happened to his friends. He wasn't sure if it was the anger or he was getting better, but he'd never opened one so fast before.

Hot, dry air wafted into Lord Gedrin's office, drifting sand on to the carpet and blowing the papers on the desk. The others who had never seen a portal before jumped back, gasping. In the distance, the walls of the fort were visible.

Mr. Tomas's face sagged, his mouth open. "No proof..." But his voice was so faint Jin could barely hear it.

Lord Gedrin stood and folded his hands. "I

disagree. I say you have no right to the property you claim, that you have taken your gems by force from a world and country with which Caerdon has no treaty, that you have conspired to hide this crime and have placed Caerdon at risk of war by your actions." He looked over at the man in the shadows. "Is the evidence sufficient, Your Grace?"

The man with the gold ring stepped forward. When Tomas saw him, he closed his eyes with a shudder, and his shoulders slumped.

"The Crown finds there is sufficient evidence of treasonous conspiracy and action on said conspiracy to bring charges against the Gariard company and all officers found to have knowledge of these actions. In view of what Metropol has discovered, we will put in motion the plan you have suggested as soon as practicable. Transport," he said, looking over Tomas with a cold expression, "will be provided for the prisoners immediately. Are they all in your hands at present?"

"They are, Your Grace."

"But what about the fort?" Jin blurted, then clapped his hands over his mouth when he realized what he had done. Now he was really in trouble. You didn't speak out of turn to nobs. Somebody had to make the *maahtik* go away, though. Why not him?

The man with the gold ring turned his cold gaze to Jin, then to Lord Gedrin. "What fort?"

"Gariard maintained an armed fort in the desert world of Darha, Your Grace," Sir Marist said when Lord Gedrin nodded to him. "You may see it through the portal. I was imprisoned in that fort for several months. Gariard people, and their armed guards, are still there."

The man stared grimly at the portal. "Then they must be dealt with. I will speak with the Prime Minister—this would be a state matter and outside my jurisdiction. I promise you, however, they will not escape my justice."

Lord Gedrin bowed, and the man with the gold ring left the room, followed by Mr. Tomas, under guard. The Metropol men, Sir Marist included, were grinning and slapping each other on the back.

Jin closed the portal before anyone complained about the wind. Then he tugged on Sir Marist's coat. "What just happened?"

"That, young Jin, was the Crown Justicar in action. No wonder Gedrin kept it secret! You see, we thought we would have to make a case for theft, or kidnapping. But someone got clever and realized what Gariard was doing was a crime against the country—treason. But you need the Crown Justicar to agree there is a case to bring a charge for treason."

Jin thought. "So they are going to go to prison?"

"Prison at the very least." Sir Marist looked grimly pleased at the thought. "I wonder how he intends to deal with the fort. Metropol is not set up for storming fortifications." He sounded as if he wished it was.

"You'd best be off, Bartly," said Lord Gedrin. "The sooner the prisoners are the Crown's responsibility rather than ours, the better. Oh, and have someone come in to sweep up the sand."

Jin hunched his shoulders. "Sorry."

Lord Gedrin raised shaggy eyebrows. "Not at all—your demonstration was most effective. Perhaps at a more convenient time you would be willing to show us more of your abilities? I am quite curious about...but that can wait. Please tell me more of this fort and how it came to be. I do apologize, Mr....?"

"Karestal," Sir Marist said.

"Mr. Karestal. We have been focused on our criminal investigation here in Thama, and frankly, the idea of travel to other worlds to find our criminals is something we've never had to consider before." Lord Gedrin's gaze went to the space where the portal had been, as if to make sure it had not come back suddenly. "No doubt you are eager to see the last of Gariard."

"The doors between worlds are a marvel to us as well." Mr. Karestal inclined his head. "It will be good to see the *maahtik* leave, but I must confess their presence was not completely evil. The *sadaak* rules Rabani, our country, but he is greedy and corrupt. He does not protect the village of Gilbadeh but only sends his tax collectors. The *maahtik* paid double taxes, and in return they were permitted to do what they wished to us. We were forced to build their fort and to serve them there. What could we do? They had the lightning sticks that killed from afar, and if they found our weapons, they took them. Our village is not rich. If you make the *maahtik* go, the taxes will not be paid, and we will be punished."

"What of this mine I heard about? Would that help pay the taxes?" Sir Marist asked.

Mr. Karestal shook his head. "Not enough, if we dig only with our hands. The *maahtik* have a metal demon that digs for them, but we do not know how to command or feed it." He frowned, his brow wrinkling with thought. "It is said...in my grandfather's time, the first of the pale strangers from Caerdon were seen. They were few, and they traded with us honestly—but when the *maahtik* came, they did not return. Perhaps they could be found and would be willing to come back and trade with us? They called themselves *vaahn-ter.*"

Jin pricked up his ears. "You mean Vanter Exotics, maybe? I found that sphere in an old burned-out Vanter building. And...and when I came through to Darha, there were boards and bricks and things in the desert. Stuff the Rabani don't have."

Lord Gedrin sat back in his chair, frowning thoughtfully. "Vanter Exotics...the name is familiar. Clearly they were jinxers—ah, I remember now. Gariard took them over some time ago. I'm afraid they are no longer in business." He glanced up at Sir Marist. "Where are we going to get jinxers of our own, eh? Looks like we're going to need them in future. Perhaps we can...but really, Gariard controls all the jinxer trade these days, and it will be hard to find one that won't be in jail once we're done with them."

"I'd rather have Jin work for us in any event," Sir Marist said. "He's quite clever and resourceful. What do you think, Jin?"

Jin squirmed, feeling his face go hot. "Don't think Metropol'd want me." They wouldn't if they knew about him, and he'd seen what they did. They liked finding things out.

"Well, we can discuss that at another time." Lord Gedrin gathered up the scattered papers on his desk. "I have a few ideas in mind that may assist your difficulties, Mr. Karestal. Mr. Tomas is not the only one with friends in the government. While we wait for word from the Crown Justicar, I will send messages...and our Investigative Devices department would like to see your demonstration again, young man. And we may as well start with your deposition concerning Gariard, Mr. Karestal."

Zinde gave Jin a meaningful glance as they left Lord Gedrin's office, so he wasn't surprised when she managed to pass him one of the extra spheres. When he was able to sneak a glance at it, it was one of the fiery gold ones that connected to Darha. He hid it in his clothes in a different place than the other two, just in case.

Sir Marist went off with the Rabani after leaving Jin at the Investigative Devices office on the second floor. Jin was suspicious at first because none of the people there looked anything like the other Metropol agents—they were all much older, and one was even a lady.

They had shelves and boxes crammed with all kinds of strange devices and machines in their offices, and they let Jin try some of them. He particularly liked the Optic Enlarger, which made the smallest details large and ordinary materials, like the cloth of his coat, seem quite strange when seen close up—like it was made of a web of huge ropes.

Mostly they just wanted to see him open portals. They all came up with new things for him to try, like making a portal through a piece of wood and seeing if anything happened to the wood afterward. Each experiment gave them more ideas, until Jin's head started hurting again.

The lady, Dr. Carell, noticed him wincing and scolded the others to stop. "You've none of you written *any* of this up in your notes yet," she said. "And we don't want to *damage* him, do we?" Then she made the harassed-looking young man who was some kind of assistant fetch Jin something called "hot chocolate," and all of the others thought that was a good idea and asked for some, too.

The assistant, who seemed to be used to this sort of thing, brought up a huge pot and some mugs. Jin liked hot chocolate very much. He also decided he liked the Investigative Devices people, even if they were a bit strange sometimes. They didn't ask Jin to open any more portals, but they studied the crystal spheres while they sipped their hot chocolate.

"It certainly *looks* like glass," one said dubiously. "But is it? And how were they made?"

"And what gave them the idea?" Dr. Carell wanted to know. "It's all very well to go *through* things, but finding other worlds—you'd think that would be somewhat difficult."

The door to the office opened, and Bartly looked in. "Ah, there you are. They want you downstairs, Jin."

"But we're not done yet!" Dr. Carell protested.

Bartly sighed. "Do you have any idea what time it is? He's been here for hours. It's nearly time for supper."

Jin said good-bye while Bartly waited patiently at the door.

"Do come back when you can. We want to try those other spheres they brought in."

"I'll try." Jin suddenly wanted to try the other spheres very badly himself. If the different colors meant different worlds, what were those worlds like?

"You shouldn't encourage them like that," Bartly said as they went back down the stairs and down the hall to Lord Gedrin's office. "They forget to eat when they're all excited by some new thing—or forget to go home at night."

Sir Marist and the Rabani were inside, discussing something very intently with Lord Gedrin.

"...no, they only want a few people there at most. We can make changes later, if everyone agrees. First, however, we need to get the Gilbadeh elders to agree. And then there is the issue of transportation."

Moro and Zinde were sitting in chairs and looking bored, but as soon as they saw Jin they sat up, eyes smiling.

"Jinli! Where did you go?"

Jin tried to explain the office of Investigative Devices.

Zinde sighed. "You were lucky. All we got to do was talk and talk and talk."

"You should like that, then." Moro dodged Zinde's halfhearted kick.

"It was boring. Everything we already knew, but we must say it all out fully, and it was written down and a red seal put on it." She tugged Jin's arm until he bent down closer, so she could speak in his ear. "I asked the woman in the kitchen for a needle and thread. I have sewed up some of the magics in my clothes and in Moro's so they can't be found easily. And I made you this." It was a small cloth bag with a string so he could hang it about his neck.

A man entered the office and handed Lord Gedrin a slip of paper. He read it, then placed it carefully on his desk. "I see we are in for another long night, but it means we can put our plans in motion." Lord Gedrin stood and gave Jin a small smile. "The message is from the Crown Justicar. The government has agreed to give us soldiers to assist us in capturing the Gariard fort—and they wish to proceed tomorrow. We'll need your help with that, Jin, so get some rest. And if you can convince Sir Marist to go home and get some rest, too, I will be very much in your debt."

Jin was so stunned he could only nod. Zinde poked Jin in the arm.

"What did he mean about the fort?"

"They are going to go and fight the *maahtik*. And put them in prison."

Zinde stared at him for a moment, her eyes glowing. Then she spun on her heel.

"Aba! I need the sword!"

CHAPTER 19
RETURN TO DARHA

Jin woke slowly, confused but not knowing why. He was warm but not lying on a thin mat. Whatever he had been sleeping on was soft and clean, and large enough he could sprawl and not feel walls or anything. He started to remember more. Was there something he was supposed to do? Where was he?

He sat up and looked around. He was in a real bed, with carved wood bedposts. Even Mr. Andel's bed hadn't been this fancy. So he wasn't at the Metropol building, then. The ceiling was dark blue, with small gold stars painted all over. Even though it was not a large room, it had its own fireplace of molded brick made to look like a castle, even with small metal flags on the towers. It reminded him of the fort.

Jin slid out of bed and wandered over to the window, where a pale sliver of light escaped the draperies. He opened them to find windows with small panes, some of them with colored glass and painted designs. The window looked down on a snow-covered courtyard with a stone fountain and plants. Off to the side he could see stone walls and more windows and steep slate roofs.

With the curtain open he could now see several pictures in frames hung on the wall. One was recognizable as a ship of some kind, but the drawing showed it half-open, so you could see inside. Another was a hot-air balloon going over mountains. The other pictures were of strange machines with gears and pulleys. Jin wondered what they did.

He started to look around for his clothes. He was wearing a huge nightshirt he didn't remember putting on, and his feet were bare. He found the shoes but couldn't find his clothes anywhere he looked in the room.

The door eased open, and a plump, grey-haired woman peered in.

"Oh, and you're up already, then." She smiled, and Jin suddenly remembered. They'd all gone in the carriage to Sir Marist's house last night. He'd been so tired he only had faint memories of what had happened, but he remembered her weeping with joy to see Sir Marist again. Mrs. Bedel, that was her name. "They'll be wanting you soon, he says. I brought you some hot water to wash up with. We've not had time to find more suitable clothing, so I hope this will do?"

She laid out clothes that, while not new, had no holes anywhere.

"But...but why? I already had clothes."

Mrs. Bedel gave him a stern look. "You're half out of those filthy old rags you were wearing, and it's not proper to run around like a scarecrow in front of all those notables—I don't care if it is an important task for the Crown! All the more reason for a clean face and a decent appearance, I say. And it isn't as if Master Janal...that is, Sir Marist needs any encouragement to go around looking like a coal drover. Now get dressed and come downstairs. Your breakfast is waiting. And don't forget to wash your face!"

She left the room, and Jin suddenly realized he was hungry. Scrambling into the clothes, he made a halfhearted attempt to clean his face before running downstairs. Not knowing where to go, he just followed his nose.

The stairs went down the side of a big, open area. Halfway down Jin realized there was a giant snake curled in the chandelier but after a moment of terror realized it was not alive. It hadn't moved or even looked at him, and there was dust on its scales. At the bottom of the stairs, Jin looked around. A big door was at one end of the room, which must be an entry hall like the one at the Metropol building. The other walls were decorated with a large skull of some strange beast, a painting of a battle, and a suit of armor with an umbrella on one arm. In the center was a large glass container with plants, taller than Jin. When he looked closer, he saw a toad inside giving him an indignant stare before it jumped away.

A hallway led away from the entry room, and the good smells came from that direction. Jin went down the hall and opened the first door he came to. He found Zinde, Mr. Karestal, Moro, and Sir Marist around a table. Several large dishes had food piled up on them, which Zinde and Moro were attacking with energy.

"Ah, Jin! Sorry for the chaos, but we're in a bit of a hurry. Just help yourself." Sir Marist went back to his conversation with Mr. Karestal. "So we could talk to this council of yours, certainly, but does anyone else have authority over your village?"

Hungry as he was, Jin just ate and paid no attention to what was being said. Then he noticed his friends were also eating as enthusiastically as he was —and they were not carefully lifting their face scarves to do it. They both had their scarves down, and so did Mr. Karestal.

"What does it mean?" Jin mumbled with his mouth full, gesturing.

Zinde grinned. It was a startling grin, now that he could see all of it and not just the way her eyes crinkled. "We do not conceal our true face from true friends," she said. "You have rescued my father, Sir Marist has brought the Metropol down on the *maahtik*....Aba says, he shows his face to you. So I do, too."

Moro looked at her and smiled. The change was not as noticeable with him, but then he had never been very careful about covering his face before.

"Where did you sleep?" Jin asked.

"A room with a large bench with a thick pad. It had pictures of flowers, little ones, all over the wall!" Zinde's hands gestured. "Aba and Moro were in another room, even bigger than mine."

How many rooms did Sir Marist's house have? Jin looked at the walls in this room. Curious objects hung from a wood railing; a telescope, a collection of small brass bells, and what looked like clocks but with only one hand and three faces. It wasn't as fancy as the Metropol building, but Jin liked it.

Jin got out of his chair to look at some of the objects and heard a distant bell. Shortly after, the door to the breakfast room opened and a man in a dark suit entered.

"Mr. Bartly is here, sir," he said, bowing.

"Right! Everybody ready?" Sir Marist pushed himself out of his chair, wincing. "Where's that blasted crutch...ah, here we are." His progress was blocked by a scowling Mrs. Bedel.

"Master Janal! Where do you think you are going? You should be in bed, resting that leg of yours, or it will never heal."

"Oh, it's not that bad—and I wouldn't miss this for the world, even if I have to crawl the entire way," Sir Marist said. "After months stuck in a stuffy cell, I am very much looking forward to extending the same courtesy to my jailers. And you don't expect Jin to go all by himself, do you?" He widened his eyes in a creditable attempt at a shocked expression.

He managed to escape while Mrs. Bedel was distracted by the change of topic. Jin and the others followed out into the entry hall.

"I could go by myself, I guess," Jin said, watching Sir Marist hobble on his crutch.

"Nonsense. Don't worry about Mrs. Bedel; she's known me all my life and still thinks I need minding. Old family servant. Ho, Bartly! Have they got the troops ready?"

Bartly was inside the coach and his usual cheerful self. "Yes, and aren't they going half mad trying to figure out if we are having a joke with them. If Lord Gedrin wasn't an old friend of the general, we'd never have pulled it off. Now here's what we want to do." He pulled out a folded paper and spread it on his knees. "First off, we want to warn the village to lie low. We'll send you through first, Mr. Karestal, and I'll go with you. After that's done, we'll send in the soldiers. We're thinking Jin can open the first portal here," he said, pointing. The paper showed a map of Thama, and over it someone had marked the location of the fort and village where they would correspond in Darha.

"Better here." Mr. Karestal tapped a different location. "It is out of sight of the fort. Do you know the leatherworker's house, Jin? Behind that." Jin nodded.

"Ah." Bartly studied the map. "I'd rather we didn't do this in the middle of the street..."

"Nearby alley, then." Sir Marist shrugged. "Or we go over a street and visit the booksellers."

Bartly snorted. "If you are trying to avoid notice, the middle of the street would be better. You may have gotten accustomed to them, but your friends are quite obviously not from around here."

They ended up using an alley. Jin felt quite at home there, and despite his worries, the portal opened easily. The warm blast of dry air told him it had worked again, but the sky beyond was dark.

"Good. No one will see you. Off you go, Bartly. We'll open the portal again in an hour."

"Wait for me, Aba!" Zinde ran up just as her father was about to leave.

He turned and shook his head. "You will stay here. No, do not argue with me. The *maahtik* still hold the fort and are a danger. Moro a'Kanahti, you will stay as well." He stepped through, and Jin closed the portal.

Zinde glared at him, and even Moro looked upset.

"The *maahtik* guards are still hunting us," Jin blurted. "Remember?"

Zinde said nothing but went back to the carriage with a peeved expression. Jin glanced at Moro, who shrugged, looking annoyed.

"It is hard for her to believe her father is rescued. Of course she wanted to stay with him. Me, I could have helped."

Jin wandered around the alley, uncertain what he should be doing. It was cold, but not nearly as uncomfortable as it could be with the coat he was wearing. He wondered if he would be allowed to keep it.

"Why did Bartly go too?" Jin finally asked Sir Marist, who was frowning and staring at the brick wall.

"To talk to the village elders about this trade proposal. We have to clean up the mess Gariard made first, of course, but what happens after that? If we can work out a way to trade, everyone will benefit."

"You mean...going to their world?" Jin felt a spike of interest, then worry. Would they expect him to help with that, too? And if he ran away to Darha, would they look for him there as well? "All the time?"

Sir Marist turned to face him, concern in his eyes. "Are you worried you will have to do it all? No such thing, I'm happy to say—well, perhaps at first. We had some interesting news concerning the prisoners while you were busy yesterday. While some of the Gariard jinxers are not trustworthy, it appears many were forced to work for the company and didn't commit any crime on their own. Once we sort out which is which, they can take over the day-to-day operations."

"Oh." Jin felt a surprising twinge of disappointment. It made sense, really. Metropol had to use him when there was nobody else, but why would they want him otherwise? Then what Sir Marist said hit him. "Metropol doesn't hire criminals? What about that twiddler that taught you?"

"By the time I'd met him, he'd already served his sentence," Sir Marist said. "It would not look well if the highest law enforcement office had an elastic view of the law, eh?"

Jin shook his head, feeling crushed. He'd started to think that maybe Metropol didn't care about the kind of crimes the billies cared about, and he could take a chance on staying and working for them a bit. He didn't know what to do now. Even Darha wouldn't be completely safe for him if there were other jinxers that could get there.

Working for Metropol would be a lot more fun than well digging. He wanted to look at more of the machines in Investigative Devices and ask Sir Marist about the things in his house and find out where the other spheres went.

"I was hoping, too, that you would have the opportunity of learning more about your abilities from the other jinxers," Sir Marist said. "Gariard has been quite careful to keep that knowledge to itself, and it would be to your advantage to pursue your talent. Metropol would, of course, be interested in anything you discover." Jin kept his head down, scuffing his feet at the cobblestones. He didn't know what to do, and he didn't know who he could ask about it, either. "I hope you have not developed a distaste for Metropol? I can readily imagine in your circumstances pleasant interactions with law enforcement are few and far between, but having worked closely with us, you may have noticed we have better manners than most billies."

"Yeah, I guess."

Sir Marist cocked his head. "Do you object to helping us now? I suppose I should have asked if you had other plans now that you are back in Thama."

"No! No, I want to help the Rabani. They're really

scared of the *maahtik*—I mean, the Gariard people at the fort. They're lots worse than the billies ever were."

"Excellent. And speaking of the Rabani..." Sir Marist took out his pocket watch. "Yes, it's about time for Bartly to report in."

Jin opened the portal again. Bartly was there, and he stepped through, wiping the sweat from his forehead and shivering as the cold air hit him.

"How did it go?"

"Oh, they're all for getting rid of the Gariard people at the fort," Bartly said, teeth chattering. "Karestal is getting his people out; he said to give him three hours and then come in. We'll have to talk more about the trade idea, but they seem well-disposed. They are not quite sure what to make of us, I think. "

Zinde ran up when the portal opened, and Sir Marist had to grab her arm to prevent her from going through.

"Just be patient a while longer, Miss Karestal. Your father would have strong words for me if I let you get in the middle of the fight. We'll go through after the soldiers do."

Zinde glared at him. "And when do we get these soldiers?"

He smiled. "We're going to collect them now."

Their carriage went several miles through Thama, to a section of warehouses on the west, across the river. They stopped in front of one of the warehouses, which unlike the others was made of stone instead of brick. The sign across the front read "Gariard."

"Why use their building? Won't they be there already, in Darha?"

"This was the place I got in from," Sir Marist said, with a wry expression. "They don't have people there unless they are expecting supplies. I very much doubt they will be expecting us—and if they are, the soldiers will deal with them."

The inside of the warehouse was not what Jin had been expecting. Instead of wood beams and rough plank floors with tall windows for light, the floor was one smooth expanse of concrete, and support was provided by iron girders. The windows he'd seen outside were opaque—the interior was lit by actual gas lamps.

It was also different because of the crowd of soldiers, some on horses, that took up most of the room inside. There was even a small cannon made of brass, on wheels and pulled by a horse in harness. The soldiers were big men in dark green uniforms, carrying rifles and packs. The group on horseback were armed with sabers and pistols. They looked serious and alert, and when Jin walked through to the front, following Sir Marist on his crutch, he could feel their curious gazes on him. Moro and Zinde huddled close to him, eyes wide and face scarves tightly wrapped.

"They are different than the *maahtik*," Zinde whispered in Rabani.

Moro nodded, swallowing hard. "I am glad they fight with us. But...will they stay friends? Or will they become like the *maahtik* in time?"

"I don't think Metropol or that Justicar man would let them," Jin said after thinking about it. "They were angry at what the *maahtik* did. And for sure Sir Marist would put a stop to it."

Moro's face cleared, and his eyes crinkled in a

smile. "*Bedu*-Marist is a true sword, indeed."

A man in a dark red uniform with gold braid on the shoulders and stripes across the front was waiting for them with his hands clasped behind his back, pacing.

"There you are." His voice was abrupt and gruff. "I hope this is not a fool's errand, Sir Marist."

"Not at all. Young Jin here will be assisting us with transportation. How do you wish to proceed, Major Sentel?"

"Cavalry scouts first, then the cannon, followed by the troops." Major Sentel glanced at Jin, eyes narrowed suspiciously, and Jin felt his stomach sink.

"Our colleague has requested we delay long enough to get all the local people free of the fort before you attack, but we can wait on the other side. You may well wish to become...acclimated. Darha is rather warm."

Major Sentel raised an eyebrow. "Is it. Very well, proceed."

Jin reached for the golden sphere in his pocket and did his best to ignore Major Sentel's skeptical expression. He clearly did not believe anything would happen. Taking a deep breath, Jin held up the sphere and focused.

It was getting easier each time. The light inside the sphere glowed, and it felt like something inside himself glowed, too. And then he heard the crackling hiss of the portal, followed by a gust of familiar dusty hot air.

The soldiers gasped and shifted, muttering. Major Sentel shouted at them to hold, his face suddenly pale. One of the horses reared, nearly unseating his rider, and the others tossed their heads and sidled away.

"Steady, Jin," Sir Marist murmured. "You're doing well."

The horses did not like the portal at all. Finally one rider dismounted and tied a blindfold around his horse's eyes and was able to lead it through. A few of the braver ones followed after that, but most had to use blindfolds. Then the soldiers started to file through, some worried, some amazed and eager.

"Can't you make that thing larger?" shouted Major Sentel. "We can barely get two at a time through."

"I'm...trying," gasped Jin. Keeping the portal open this long was hard enough. He wasn't even sure how to make it larger.

"Try harder, boy!"

"You are welcome to make the attempt yourself, Major." Sir Marist's voice had the coldness that meant he was angry, even if the words were polite. Major Sentel glared at him but made no response.

Jin was feeling dizzy by the time the last soldier went through. Zinde was right on his heels, followed by Moro. Sir Marist hobbled through, and he and Moro pulled Jin through to a stone room with drifts of sand in the corners and bright light streaming through big double doors.

He was back in Darha. Jin let the portal collapse with a sigh of relief.

CHAPTER 20
JIN FINDS A HOME

They watched the fight for the fort from the roof of the Gilbadeh council building. Sir Marist had a small brass telescope that they took turns using. The elders of the council were there, too, with someone holding a large umbrella-like shade on a pole. Zinde's parents had disapproved, but when she insisted on staying, they remained with her. Une Karestal had hugged Jin the instant she saw him, even tugging down her face scarf to kiss his cheek.

Major Sentel had recovered from his surprise at suddenly finding himself in a desert and gone straight to work. The cavalry scouts had first surrounded the fort from the dunes, and when the cannon and foot soldiers arrived, they split off and headed for the mines. The sound of distant gunfire came from that direction, but only briefly.

The fort gates were shut and the walls manned, at least at first. The Caerdon soldiers were quick to pick off any of the fort guards that showed themselves, and once the guards were pinned down, the cannon was wheeled up.

It took four cannonballs to take out the gate. A small group of green-coated soldiers ran through the smoke to the arch of the gate and past the shattered wood of the doors, and not long after that, Jin saw through the telescope a green uniform on the top of the fort wall.

"Excellent!" Sir Marist said, gazing through the telescope himself. "Please inform our hosts the fort has been taken."

The news was greeted with stunned surprise and then shaky smiles, as if the elders could not quite believe they were finally free of the *maahtik*. Zinde whooped and held up a hand for the telescope.

"Ha! The *maahtik* come out with their hands bound. See the miserable ones, how they hang their heads in shame and fear!"

"What will be done with them?" Moro asked.

"Since they have committed crimes against the Crown, they'll be taken back to Thama and put on trial," Sir Marist said once this had been translated.

Moro had a serious expression on his face. "Here, too, they have done evil. Many Gilbadehi have died at their hands. It is a matter of blood-honor."

Sir Marist shut the telescope and put it away in a pocket. "Then they should be tried and punished appropriately. I do not have the authority to make promises, but it may well be we can agree to have them tried for those crimes in our courts as well." He glanced at Jin, smiling. "Are you feeling strong enough for another portal? I'd like to get this lot back to Thama as soon as possible."

By the time the first batch of prisoners had gone through the portal, Jin was starting to shake with fatigue, and Major Sentel reluctantly agreed to stop for the night. As they walked back to the village, Jin saw crowds of people, more than he had ever seen outside before, talking and laughing. If any of the Gilbadehi saw one of the green-coated soldiers, they swarmed him and offered spiced tea or little cakes—

the jinli of his nickname. The soldiers looked confused but pleased, and everyone tried to communicate with gestures or just smiling a lot. It seemed to work.

Jin found Sir Marist in the council building, sitting on a rug at a low table and talking with great animation with the council elders. Mr. Karestal and Zinde were busily translating.

"So I understand this *sadaak* fellow is the actual ruler, but you don't see much of him."

One of the elders made a sour face, as if he had bitten into something that tasted bad. "His army is not seen more than a day's march from Bos-Vedai. Only his tax collectors go farther. We asked for aid when the *maahtik* first came, but they bribed the *sadaak,* and he left them there to torment us. They pay the tax and do not interfere elsewhere; the *sadaak* cares for nothing else."

Sir Marist rubbed his chin, looking thoughtful. "I'd really rather not start a war here, but we can't count on the *sadaak* remaining in ignorance."

Jin dropped to the carpet beside Sir Marist. "We could if we fooled him," he said. "Pretend the Gariard people never left? Oh, but I guess he'd want that tax money anyway."

The council elders muttered to each other, smiling. "It is a clever idea. The tax money...we can do as the *maahtik* did, and take gemstones from the mines and trade them to the a'Tema."

"The slaves in the mines were freed," Zinde whispered in Jin's ear, "but many have nowhere to go. The a'Tema say they will teach them how to use the machine that digs and to mine safely so they do not die. We will pay them for the work, while they live with us."

"I agree. A very tidy solution. The *sadaak* has no need to know the details. No doubt he would think all foreigners look the same, anyway." Sir Marist sighed. "We'll get the diplomats involved now, but we've covered the important matters."

"It is so." The head elder gestured with his white fan. "Let us now celebrate the victory and the alliance of a'Tema and Gilbadeh, and feast with our new friends."

Jin was not sure he had enough strength to move, but fortunately the feast was held in the council hall, and he didn't have to. More cushions and low tables were brought in, and what looked like the entire town came in bearing food. He ate until he was stuffed. There were chickens stuffed with dried fruit, rice dusted with spices, and little round balls of fried dough with meat inside. Everything was delicious, and when all the plates were empty, bowls of chilled, honeyed fruit were placed on the tables.

"How does it get cold?" Jin asked.

Moro grinned. "A secret of the well diggers. There is a way to make the cold air of the *kanah* stay, deep in the earth, and they store the fruit there." He hesitated, his eyes shifting away. "Are you going to come back and dig wells with us now? Now that the *maahtik* are gone?"

Zinde's eyes sparkled with happiness. "Yes, Jinli! Now you can stay, and you don't *have* to be a well digger to hide anymore. Although...although I would like to see this *ocean* you told us of in Galetan."

Moro looked thoughtful, nodding agreement.

"I don't know...I don't know what I am doing now." He leaned closer, whispering, "They will have other jinxers! And they will be going back and forth to Thama, too. I just wanted the *maahtik* to go away so everyone would be safe here."

Zinde frowned.

"Get ready to run," Moro said. "When Zinde is silent, an earthquake follows after." He flinched, expecting a punch, but Zinde just gave him a look of lofty scorn.

"It is honor between friends to speak truth to one another. To my father, Sir Marist is a friend so close his face is shown. Why do you not trust him, Jinli?"

"It is different for us. I think...I think he is a friend, but he is a man of the law. He has to do what it says."

Zinde rose to her feet. "That is stupid. I will speak with him and make him understand."

Panic froze Jin in place. "Zinde! No!"

"Earthquake," Moro said. He put a pillow over his head. "Did I not warn you? What are you worried about, anyway?"

It probably would take an earthquake to stop Zinde, Jin decided. He watched with despair as Zinde went up to the table where Sir Marist was sitting, waving her hands and talking rapidly. Then he saw Sir Marist was trying to get up, despite his injured leg, and decided to go over himself and get it over with. He didn't want Moro to know. He didn't want anyone to know. Zinde was only trying to help. *It was going to happen eventually.*

"Thank you, Jin. It was not difficult at all to sit *down*, but my leg is still not quite to the point of easily allowing me to stand again. Now, what is the difficulty? Miss Karestal seems to feel you are in some sort of danger and wants me to deal with it—but perhaps I misunderstood?" Jin hesitated, not sure what to say. Zinde hadn't told Sir Marist everything, then. "I know something has been troubling you, Jin. Do you wish to speak to me in private? I assure you I will respect your confidences."

"You can't. Not...not if it's Metropol stuff, right?"

"Ah. Am I to assume this might be a potential criminal matter?" Jin nodded, unable to speak. Sir Marist didn't seem angry or anything. He looked interested. "Well, aside from the absence of any evidence...perhaps we could discuss it in hypothetical terms."

"Hypo...whatsis?"

Sir Marist's lips twitched. "That means you will describe to me what *someone you heard of* did. If, for example, a crime was committed, I would be obliged to find this other person to arrest them. What...sort of crime did this nameless person do?"

"Embezzlement." Sir Marist blinked but nodded at Jin to continue. Slowly Jin told the whole story of Mr. Andel and the burial money, making sure to speak of "someone he heard of" and not naming any names.

"Forgive me...but how did you ever come across the term embezzlement?"

"It was on a poster in that billy bin you sent me to. I asked the billy what it meant, and he told me. Taking money someone trusted you with."

"I'm not a lawyer, but I do have some knowledge of the law, being an agent of Metropol," Sir Marist said. "And law is always about the details. This billy told you the truth, Jin, but he left out a few important parts. For one thing, embezzled money is used for the embezzler's *personal* benefit. From what you have said, this hypothetical individual didn't keep as much as a penny. Rather, the whole sum was given as directed to pay for the burial. I'm afraid I don't see a crime here."

"Oh." Suddenly Jin found himself sitting hard on the floor. His head was buzzing. He wasn't a thief at all. Sir Marist had said so, and he was like...like a billy for billies.

"Who was it, Jin?" Sir Marist said gently.

"Mr. Andel. I would bring his food when he was sick. He was real kind to me. He showed me how to read the books he had and told me about Vanter Exotics and all sorts of things. Sometimes... sometimes when it was really cold, he'd ask me to sleep on the foot of his bed, so his feet wouldn't get chilled." Even as he spoke, Jin realized Mr. Andel had done it to help Jin just as much as himself. How had he not seen that before? "He told me I shouldn't steal...but Ogney was going to steal it, for real, and...it was what he wanted. Even if it was wrong, I would have done it anyway, for him."

"Quite right."

Zinde sighed heavily. "Then Jinli can stay with us now? He has no home, no family. Moro will mope if Jinli goes away and complain to *me*. My mother will worry about him."

Moro, hearing his name, looked up and came closer.

"Why do you disturb our guest, troublesome daughter of Karestal?" asked the head elder. "Have you not spoken enough today?"

Zinde ducked her head. "*Wasa, aba-Gilbadeh.* I must still speak. What has been decided concerning Jinli? He has no home and no kinfolk in his world. If not for him, the *maahtik* would still be here. It is village-honor, and...and family-honor, too!" She glanced at her father.

"It is as you say, Zinde a'Karestal. We owe Jinli much. Hasnen a'Kanahti has already offered to take Jinli in as a son, but Jinli is of the world of Galetan, and his people should be consulted before this is done." The elder gestured at Sir Marist.

Moro's eyes widened in surprise, and then he hit Jin on the shoulder, grinning. "Ha! I will have a younger brother with a face like cheese! Oh, the shame of it!"

"Exceeded only by the shame of an older brother who moves like mud," Jin instantly replied, grinning back.

"We...had also thought to do this. Our debt is even greater, for he saved my life," said Mr. Karestal.

The elder nodded, frowning. "This is also true. But what can be done? A child cannot be son to two families at the same time."

Zinde had been whispering in Sir Marist's ear the whole time, translating, and now he looked at Jin with a slight smile.

"Well, Jin? What do you want to do? Metropol and Caerdon are in your debt, too, and I am rather pleased myself you saw fit to rescue me. We could argue for hours about who owes you more, but perhaps we should find out what you would like instead. I believe between us we can make it happen, whatever it is."

It was hard to speak. "I guess...I'd like to be in both Darha and Galetan," Jin said hesitantly. "I want to learn more about being a jinxer. And I want to help Gilbadeh, too. You don't have put me in a family, though. I can manage. Have so far, anyway."

"You have to have *some* family," Zinde said, shocked. "How will people know how to greet you? To Rabani it is not right to have no kin at all." She grinned. "Only demons have no kin. And when the people hear what you did, they will want your name among us!"

Before Jin could stop her, Zinde proceeded to tell everyone in earshot her version of the burial money, also describing the dangerous streets of Thama that she had seen and the other wonders, like the river.

"Earthquake," Moro said, handing Jin a pillow. "There is nothing to be done about it."

The council murmured to each other for a moment when she had finished, then the head elder spoke.

"Jinli acted as a son to this Andel, obeying his wishes even at risk to himself, from a true thief. We suggest this—let Jinli be in truth the son of Andel, in our law. And let him be considered kin to both Karestal and Kanahti, in recognition of their debt to him."

Sir Marist nodded. "Well done. All parties satisfied."

Mr. Karestal also appeared happy. "Do you understand what that means, Jinli? You are always welcome in our home, and in the home of a'Kanahti. Our faces our shown to you, your troubles are ours. You are not alone anymore. Stay with us as you wish."

Jin tried to smile, but it felt a little wobbly. "I guess I will, since I don't really have any place to stay in Thama."

"Actually, you do," Sir Marist interrupted. "You've seen my house; I could put up half the village there and never notice. Besides, if you are there to be fussed over, Mrs. Bedel won't be worrying about me. I would consider it a favor on your part."

"But...but you're a nob! Nobs don't house gutter rats like me," Jin protested, trying not to think of the wonderful devices and strange rooms—and the toad house—in Sir Marist's home.

Sir Marist gave him a disbelieving look. "Jin Andel, were you listening at any point with all that chatter in Lord Gedrin's office the previous day? This trade agreement with Darha isn't some little private affair. The *Crown* is taking charge, and right now you are the only jinxer we have. Ergo, royal jinxer, although they will probably come up with some crusty title nobody can pronounce later on...*but*, the point remains, you require housing suitable to your station. One hopes the room you were given was adequate? It used to be mine, and I'm afraid some of my youthful alchemical experiments left their marks on the furnishings."

Jin grinned and nodded.

"And of course there is room should your friends wish to visit. To see oceans and the like."

Zinde gaped at Sir Marist, silenced for once in her life. Moro nudged her, looking worried at this unusual circumstance, and she shook herself and immediately started telling him what had been said.

Jin sat and listened to his friends happily make plans to explore Galetan. And maybe they could all explore other worlds, too. He had family now, and work to do.

This was going to be fun.

ABOUT THE AUTHOR

Sabrina Chase used to spend a great deal of time worrying about Entropy and the heat death of the Universe, but the pay was better in software development. It also provides time for her fiction habit. She resides in the soggy Pacific Northwest under proper feline supervision.
More information for the curious is available at chaseadventures.com

9 781940 006147